Young Lincoln

Jan Jacobi

Library of Congress Control Number: 2017934685

ISBN: 9781681061122

Printed in the United States of America
18 19 20 21 22   5 4 3 2 1

Dedication

For my students, past and present.

Table of Contents

Preface

I am an unlikely fellow.

No one would have thought I'd end up president. I didn't think so myself. When my friends first approached me and said I should run, I said, "Just think of such a sucker as me as president."

When Molly first came to Springfield to live with her sister Elizabeth, she told everyone she was going to marry a president. Of course, that was when Douglas was sweet on her, and she thought she'd catch him.

She married me instead. She always called me "Mr. Lincoln," but I'm sure she never thought she'd call me "Mr. President."

As a boy, I loved to read the fables of Aesop. Those tales really set how I thought about the world. They were simple stories, mostly about animals, but I learned to crack them open like a walnut to get what was inside. I learned that if a story was told right, it could make a point without trying.

Years later I realized there was one about me that everyone knows—the tortoise and the hare. There's more to it than people think. You have to look at it closely. Here was this ugly, old, plodding tortoise telling this showoff hare that he could beat him in a race. It was sort of like when I challenged Douglas to those debates in '58.

Without saying it, people were always telling me I was that tortoise. One fellow told me I was so ugly I had no business running for the state legislature. I was called "two-faced" so often that I replied, "If I had another one, do you think I'd be wearing this face?"

But the tortoise just kept at it.

I never thought of being president, and I still don't.

Twice I lost when I ran for the Senate. It was getting so I was proudest of being elected captain of my company in the Black Hawk War.

The most I'd say for myself is that I became an instrument of purpose. Whether I'd been that all my life, I can't say. I sure never saw myself that way, and neither did anyone else. Some of those people in Salem would have said, "He jes' loafs around readin' his books all day. Ain't no good a-comin' of him."

All I knew was I didn't want to be a farmer.

PART ONE

Kentucky, Indiana, and Illinois

Chapter One

Tied Together by Opposites

My childhood's home I see again,
And sadden with the view;
And still, as memory crowds my brain,
There's pleasure in it too.

Papa sat on the hearthstone stool and peered into the fireplace. He was squat but very strong. His face was round with a large nose, and he had golden-brown eyes. His hair was stiff and deep black. When he looked into the fire, he was quiet and withdrawn, but he loved to tell stories, and the one we heard most was how Uncle Mord had saved his life.

"I was six and Mama was off by the neighbors. It was spring and we was planting the corn—Pappy, Mord, Josiah, and me. We wasn't far from our cabin. The farm was closed in from the giant hick'ry and oak trees that was right up to the field. It always felt dark even on a sunshiny day.

"Mord was fourteen and helping Pappy, Josiah followed Mord, but I was throwing stones at the birds.

"'Tommy, quit your foolin' and get back to your chores,' says Mord, but Pappy tells him, 'Let him be, Mordecai.'

"It was real quiet. We wasn't worried much about anything. We'd knowed that panthers and wolves had once been around, but no one had seed a panther since the pioneers come.

"I seed a flash from behind the bushes and then I heard a loud crack. Pappy looked afeard, his eyes rolled, and he went down flat in the dirt. His brains, which was white, was out from the back of his head where the red blood was gushing.

"'Indians!' yelled Mord, and he tells Josiah, 'Go to the stockade and git help.' Then he hightailed it to the cabin.

"The savage jumps out from the brush and rushed over to us. I was so scared with that huge savage squatting over me and Pappy lying face down where we had laid the corn seeds. I just cried and cried. Far as I could tell he was going to take me into them woods. His face was red and it was painted black, white, and green. Feathers hanged down from the back of his head, and his chest was bare but for a silver trinket that was dangling over his heart.

"His hands was almost on me when I heard another crack, and that silver piece went flying and the savage's chest bust open, covering me with his blood. He went down harder than Pappy and right next to him.

"There was other savages, but when they seed what happened and heard another crack from the gun, they beat it back into the woods.

"Mord, he told me later, he git to the cabin, fetch the rifle, and plug that savage with one shot. If I don't know no better, I don't know how Mord done it.

"The soldiers from the stockade come to rescue us, but it was Mord done all the work.

"That's how I lost my Pappy, and that's how you git your name, Abe. Abraham, from Pappy, that was killed dead by that savage."

When I was two and we were living in Kentucky, we moved from the cabin where I was born in Nolin and settled on land near Knob Creek. Papa thought he'd make it a farm. He cut the wood for the cabin, and the neighbors came for a gathering and helped him build it.

Right in front of our cabin ran the Cumberland Valley Trail. It's hard to picture since where we lived in

5

Kentucky was so isolated. Our part of the trail ran from Nashville to Louisville. Some of the travelers would stop to talk to us. There were people migrating west looking for something better. Why, Dan'l Boone himself, who we were supposedly related to, might have moseyed past Knob Creek.

The cabin was dark and close. There was one small window, and the door, which was a warped board, creaked on its rawhide hinges. The light clawed its way through the cracks in the logs, and it flooded the cabin when one of us opened the door. At night, shadows from the yellow-orange glow of the fire prowled around us.

Four of us lived in that one small room. It smelled of drying meat, cooking grease, smoke, animal hides, and stale sweat. The floor was dirt; there were no chairs, just stools; the table was makeshift; and our beds were on poles pushed into cracks in the cabin wall. The chimney was on the outside, and it was made of clay and sticks.

At night we gathered around the hearth of the fireplace. Sometimes it was to help Mama with the cooking, but in the winter it was for the heat. Our food was from the corn and potatoes we could harvest after the growing season, and from whatever squirrels, rabbits, and deer Papa could shoot. Mama mixed it all together in a stew she cooked in a large pot with long legs that she called her Dutch oven. One night the only thing on the supper table was roasted potatoes. Papa muttered, "May these blessings fit us for thy service in Christ's name," but all I could think was they were a mighty poor blessing.

Our clothes were pretty ragged. Mama made shirts of linsey for Sarah and me to wear in the warmer weather, and Papa and I had denim pants with foxing to cover the tears. In the winter it was very cold. We'd wear woolen shirts that Mama spun and wove, but they wore out fast. The hide on my buckskin jacket stiffened and cracked before I could outgrow it. I remember when my toes stuck out through my broken shoes. When my arms were out at the elbows, I shivered with the cold.

Papa was a carpenter. He scratched by on odd jobs. He did that all his life. He never went to school, he could barely read, and he never did more in the way of writing than smudge his own name. He wasn't much of a farmer, and he cleared just enough land for us to get by. He liked to hunt, but he also set traps all over our little place.

Once I came across a bear cub in one of his traps. It wasn't very big, but it had scraped its shins to the bone trying to free itself from the rusted metal pincers. Pools of blood, smeared with flakes of rust and patches of black hair, lay on the ground. Every few moments, the bear moaned and then cried out helplessly. When I came closer, suddenly its eyes, which had been rolling upward, focused directly on me. I felt it begging me to let it die without having to suffer the frightful pain any longer.

I knew what Papa would do to me if I set it free, but I never gave it a second's thought. I reached down carefully and unsnapped the clasp that held it tight. The bear collapsed on the ground when I pulled it from the trap. We were quiet for a time, both of us breathing heavily. I reached down, scooped the limp body into my arms, and carried it into the woods.

I laid it in the hollow of a huge oak tree and slowly walked back to our cabin. The next day when I returned, it was gone. Somehow Papa knew what I had done, and he wailed me hard for it. There was no mercy in him. Mama understood me more than he did. She wouldn't have thrashed me for it.

Mama was taller than Papa. She had gray eyes, which she passed on to me, and some say I got her looks. All the cooking, spinning, sewing, and washing wore her down. She was thin, and her bones stuck out a bit.

Mama was smart and knew how to read a little. If it was the Bible, she could read just fine. She was always telling us stories about the people who lived in Israel.

She was always kind. It was what the neighbors most said about her. After we were in Indiana and the milk-sick came, she sat with her aunt and uncle Sparrow when they were dying, and she would walk a half mile to be with Mrs. Brooner.

Her mother was not married when Mama was born, and she never told Mama about her father. Mama was raised by Uncle Thomas and Aunt Betsy Sparrow. She was unhappy sometimes. When she felt like that, she didn't want to see much of the neighbors. Every so often, when I looked over at her while she was cooking dinner, I could see that her eyes were empty and sad.

—

Sometimes I felt sad myself. I would walk over the hills, which were made out of limestone and covered with sassafras, redbud, and sycamore trees. I walked down into the valley where Knob Creek trickled toward the Rolling Fork River.

Most times I would hear the cardinals calling "cheer, cheer" or "wick-er, wick-er" to each other and see the red darts diving through the thick green leaves. The sun dappled through the tops of the trees onto the darker pockets of brush below. When the trail dipped down, it might lead to a woodland creek. The cold water trickled through my toes and glittered like silver in the morning sun. The sadness left, and I could believe I was in that garden in the Bible.

Our Knob Creek farm lay in a valley that rose toward the steep hills. Cutting into the sides of the valley were deep gorges. There wasn't much land for growing crops. Papa had cleared three fields from the trees and the brush near our cabin. He plowed them each spring to loosen the soil and prepare it for the planting. I trailed Papa and the horse, breaking up some of the larger clods with my small hoe.

One Saturday afternoon, while Papa and some of the neighbors' boys were planting the corn in the big field, he let me build little mounds where he told me to plant the pumpkin seeds. I carefully rounded the soil for each of the tiny hills, leveled off the top, laid each seed in the soil at the proper depth, and then covered it gently with the loose dirt. Papa told me I was making too much fuss and that the plants didn't care whether everything was just right.

"Abe," he said, "you jes' forgit about them seeds and next thing you know they'll be up."

When we walked back to the cabin, Papa said it felt like rain.

That night I heard the thunder, but I went back to sleep because there was no rain. In the morning, I ran out to the field to see whether my seeds had come up even though Papa had said it wouldn't be right away.

I couldn't believe what I saw. My hills, along with all my seeds, had been washed away!

I heard Papa calling from the other side. He was looking at each of the rows with the corn seeds, where the same thing had happened.

"Abe, it done happened again. I should have known. It sure showed me it was going to let loose. It rained up in them hills and the water run down the valley. It flooded in from them gorges and spilled across our land. It took our seeds and all our hard work with it."

Papa could see that I was going to cry, so he gave me a hug and said we'd just have to start over.

One morning during the summer when I was six, I trotted off into the woods with my dog, Honey, for company. When he was with me, I never felt lonesome. We explored every trail in the forest, and sometimes we'd even get off the path. Honey always led me home, so Mama and Papa never worried about us.

We'd be on the lookout for rabbits, which Honey liked to chase. Honey once cornered one in an old elm tree. His fur was up, and he barked furiously at the base of the tree. He kept nosing as deep as he could into that hole, growling and baring his teeth. He emerged with a mouthful of fur, which he tossed aside in disgust. He was bent on killing that old rabbit.

I was bound for the fishing hole with my pole and some worms that I'd dug up behind the cabin. It wasn't far, and Honey ran ahead because he seemed to know where we were going. It was a place where the creek was stopped up by some brush the beavers had built. In the early morning or late afternoon, I could sometimes see the fish rising to catch the flies that drifted toward the water.

I plopped my line into the pool, and Honey and I sat patiently on the bank. I listened to the birds calling and the leaves rustling gently in the breeze.

We hadn't sat long before my pole dipped toward the water, and after a few tugs, a small fish flapped furiously across the surface. Honey's shrill bark pierced the morning air. As I pulled it in, I could see it was a small bluegill. Mama would fry it up, and we'd have it for dinner.

I didn't get another bite, so both Honey and I grew restless. I packed up, put the fish in the tin can with the worms, and then we eased along the path home. From a distance, I could see that Papa was talking to a man by the wooden fence in front of the cabin. It was probably a stranger who had been walking along the Cumberland Valley Trail.

When we got closer, I could see that his clothes were tattered and that he had a rifle slung over his shoulder.

He was taller than Papa, and he had an ugly wound on his neck that looked like it had recently healed. His face was weathered and wrinkled.

"Abe," said Papa, "this feller is come from New Orleans where he fit with Andy Jackson. He's on his way to Louisville to see some relations."

"Just happy to be alive, young man," said the stranger.

I gasped, "Were you really there?"

"Indeed, I was," he replied.

I climbed onto the top rail of the fence to get closer.

"Indeed, I was. Regular army, militia, free Negroes, Choctaws, and the pirate Jean Lafitte and his men, it was all of us against the British, and we were outnumbered. We dug a steep rampart and called it Line Jackson. On top was Old Hickory himself, with his sword drawn, yelling, 'Give it to them, my boys. Let us finish the business today.'

"That's just what we did. Polished them off in thirty minutes. Two thousand of them down and only one hundred of us. They surrendered and the war was done."

I was so excited to see this soldier and hear about the war that I blurted, "We've had soldiers in our family. They were in the War for Independence."

"Reckon they must be your grandparents," he observed.

Papa gave him the lowdown. "My Uncle Jacob fit in the Battle of Brandywine Creek, and his relative, Hananiah Lincoln, was with Gen'ral Washington at Yorktown."

"No, Papa, you ain't got it right. It's the other way around."

Papa's face turned bright red. He moved like a panther and gave me a shove, sending me over backwards. I cracked my back and my head as I hit the ground.

"Ain't I told you enough times not to interrupt me? And you won't ever be saying I ain't right."

When I climbed back up, I did my best to hide my tears.

Papa and the soldier continued their jawing about the war and the soldier's time in the Tennessee militia. They got on to the time Papa drifted down the rivers to New Orleans on a flatboat and about the murderers and pirates that lived in the Cave-in-Rock on the Ohio River.

"You done heard about them Harpe brothers?" asked Papa.

"I have indeed," replied the stranger.

"We knowed enough to stay away from them Harpe women on the bank, but Bill McRoby fell for it and said he'd rescue them," Papa said with a scowl.

"And he was robbed?"

"He was."

"And murdered?"

"He was."

"How unfortunate!" he exclaimed. "Down in Orleans, I heard they got rid of the Harpes because they stripped someone naked, tied him to a horse, and shoved him and the horse off the bluff."

"Yup, I heard that one too," said Papa.

I remembered about my fish and that Papa and Mama had always taught me to honor the soldiers. I got down, pulled the little bluegill out of the tin can, and presented it to the soldier.

Taking it in his hands, he said, "Why, young man, that's plenty thoughtful of you."

"Papa, can Mama fix it for him for dinner? Maybe he can stay with us and tell us more about Andy Jackson."

"Well, Abe, I sometimes cain't figger if you is the same boy. I was about to tar you, and now you done what your mama and me been trying to learn you."

If Papa said he couldn't figger me, it was hard for me to understand him too. You could just never be sure about him. It was much easier being with my friend Austin, who lived nearby.

To get to Austin's house, I had to walk a stretch through the woods. Austin was my best friend. He was three years older, but since I was tall for my age, we were about the same height. We played together in the woods and the creek as often as we could.

Austin let on he was afraid when he walked through the woods by himself. He was worried about the animals, particularly the snakes. I could understand how Austin felt. The trail was narrow, and we'd gotten lost before. Sometimes a big buck would crash through the underbrush, or a bobcat might threaten and hiss at us. Once a rattlesnake fell out of a rise onto the trail, but even though it coiled to strike us, I wasn't afraid. Austin wanted to run away, but I told him not to move. After we froze for some minutes, it just slithered away.

The worst thing I could conjure up would be getting lost in the dark. That happened once, and we just laid down in the leaves under the bushes. Austin was shaking most of the night from the cold or the noises of the creatures, but somehow when I saw the moon poking through the trees, I felt better. I tried to calm Austin and we made it through the night.

On the days the creek swelled, Austin and I played all day in the water. One day we were supposed to be hunting for turkeys, at least Austin was, but we waded into the creek and felt the current carrying us away. It was a strong pull. Neither of us could swim, but we ignored Mama's warnings.

At one crossing, Austin said, "Let's play coon," and one foot after the other, he balanced himself on a fallen tree trunk and crept across the rapids. When it came my turn to "coon," I got halfway, but my foot slipped, and I splashed down into the whirlpool of white, rushing water.

It pulled me under, and I couldn't touch the rocks and sand in the creek bed. I paddled frantically and was able to keep my head above the water, but after each desperate stroke, it rushed back over me. I could hear Honey barking wildly and Austin screaming at me, but I could not gather what he was yelling. As I gasped for breath, I knew that Papa and Mama were nowhere near. My strength was ebbing.

If it had continued much longer, I might have given up, but I felt a sturdy poking in my side.

I could barely hear Austin yelling, "Git it and hold on."

Again, there was a poking, this time in my right shoulder. With what effort I had left, I pushed above the water and saw Austin holding a large sycamore branch and extending it toward me. I turned and grasped it tightly. Gradually, Austin was able to pull me out of the swirling waters and over toward the side of the creek. I was overjoyed to be able to stand on the bottom of the creek once more.

I coughed hard and then laid out on the grass. As I rested and felt the sun warming me, suddenly I sat up and said to Austin, "Now I got another worry. What will Mama do?"

"She'll skin you for goin' in when you shouldn't because your clothes is all wet," he said.

"What kin we do?"

"We'll put your clothes on that branch to dry, and then we'll tell your mama we was lost."

I didn't like the idea of not telling Mama the truth, but I couldn't see any other way out. And it wasn't really a lie because we were always getting lost in the woods— just not that day.

In the late fall, after we'd helped our families with the harvest, Austin and I went to Zachariah Riney's blab school and then to the one where Caleb Hazel was the teacher. We called them "blab schools" because of all the noise we made when we were reciting our lessons.

One day when we were walking home, Austin suddenly said, "Abe, ain't you asked old Riney about that book, *Robinson Crusoe?*"

"Yup," I said.

"Why that one so bad?"

"Old Riney likes it. He says it's about a feller that goes on a boat and gits himself shipwrecked. He gits stuck on some island," I responded.

"Ain't this Robinson Crusoe where Riney says he calls his friend Friday?"

"Yup, that's what old Riney says."

"Well, what I don't git is why he ain't called him Saturday. Saturday's a better day than Friday. If I'd git to name a friend after a day, I'd call him Saturday."

Austin was always full of strange notions like this.

One afternoon after school, some of the older boys ganged up on Austin and me and made fun of us. They taunted me about my clothes. Mama always sent me off in a long-tail linsey shirt and Sarah's sun hat. When Austin told them off, they shoved us into the dirt and started to pummel us. I broke free and was ready to fight.

The biggest boy went after me first. He punched at me wildly, but all I had to do was duck. I hit him with my right fist, and he dropped to the ground. Blood dripped from his nose and mouth onto the dirt.

I learned something about myself early. Although I was wiry, I had Papa's strength. I was starting to do harder chores like carrying in the firewood and helping Papa to plow. And something else. When a fight started and everyone else was getting riled up, for some reason I stayed calm.

Austin didn't like school because the only thing he could think about was hunting. We explored every hill and valley in our neighborhood. I did the scouting and he did the shooting. Somehow I didn't like killing things.

We wondered about who might have passed along the Cumberland Valley Trail and whether their ghosts were still there. He was sure that Indians must have lived in our valley and that once a year their spirits came back to hunt for deer. I didn't put much stock in ghosts, but Austin, who had a fertile imagination, cooked up some good stories.

Once at midnight, when the wind was up, we snuck out into his woods to see if it was the Indians' time. We hunkered down, and Austin whispered that he saw something moving. Just as I started to tell him he was stretching it, there was a rush of air, something sweeping past us, and then a thrashing on the ground and high-pitched squeaks. We had no idea what it was, but since we figured we might be next, we got out of there like a couple of rabbits being chased by Honey.

———

Although we had good times, it seemed the bad times were always around. Mama's belly started to swell. My sister Sarah was so excited; she was the one to tell me that Mama was going to have a baby. Sarah was two years older, so she understood better what was happening. For me, having a younger brother to play with sounded just fine.

When Mama's time came, there was a woman to help her. Papa sent me away to Austin's, but he and Sarah were there and heard Mama's cries. Sarah told me afterward it made her afraid for her own time someday.

At the end, there was squalling from our baby brother, who was named Thomas after Papa.

Right from the start we knew something was wrong. Mama was in bed the whole time trying to get the baby to feed. He didn't last but a few days. The sadness came so quick.

Papa took me out and showed me how we were to make little Thomas his coffin. I had never seen Papa so sad, but somehow shaping and building that little box helped him feel better.

We carried Thomas in his little box up one of the hills. If ever you'd want to be in a pretty spot for eternity, this was it. Papa dug the place, we laid Thomas in the earth, and then we walked back home.

That winter, Sarah and I were lying on the cabin floor next to the fireplace. It was after supper and Mama was reading to us from the Bible. Soon we would go to sleep. The light from the flames flickered across her face and over the yellow-brown pages of the aging book. She held its dried leather cover delicately in her worn and wrinkled hands. Her strong, deep voice carried us off into the land of Canaan.

And Abraham took the wood of the burnt offering, and laid it upon Isaac his son; and he took the fire in his hand, and a knife; and they went both of them together. . . . And Isaac spake unto Abraham his father, and said, My father . . . Behold the fire and the wood: but where is the lamb for a burnt offering? And Abraham said, My son, God will provide himself a lamb for a burnt offering: so they went both of them together.

And they came to the place which God had told him of; and Abraham built an altar there, and laid the wood in order, and bound Isaac, his son, and laid him on the altar upon the wood. And Abraham stretched forth his hand, and took the knife to slay his son. And the angel of the Lord called unto him out of heaven, and said, Abraham, Abraham . . . Lay not thine hand upon the lad, neither do thou any thing unto him: for now I know that thou fearest God, seeing thou hast not withheld thy son, thine only son from me.

She closed the book and looked into the fire. Sarah was next to me and laid her arm over my shoulders. No one spoke. All we could hear was the hissing from the logs.

"Mama," I asked, "why does Abraham want to kill Isaac?"

"He don't want to kill him, Abe," she said slowly. "He almost done it because God told him to."

"But why would God tell him to do it?"

"It's as the Book says, Abe. God was a-testin' him."

"But why would God do that?"

"He is a-testin' us, even the little ones like you, every day. There ain't nothin' that ain't in the Book."

"But, Mama, it ain't right. God shouldn't be telling Abraham to kill Isaac."

"It ain't up to you, Abe."

"What if God told Papa to do it to me? What would Papa do? What if God didn't stop him?"

"Abe, there's worries a-plenty without fixing a notion on God and his ways."

"But, Mama, Isaac must have been so skeered. What was he thinking about his pappy? I don't care if it is in the Book, Mama, it just ain't right."

———

What I was learning was that my world was made up of things that were pulling against each other. Sometimes Mama was happy, but then at other times, for no reason, she seemed deeply sad. It was also that way with me: pleasure was tinged with sadness. Papa could be kind to me, but then he was also mean and thrashed me. He lit up for strangers like the soldier, but then he lit into me. Our baby Tommy died, but God stopped Abraham from killing Isaac and he lived. I mostly liked being alone, but then I liked being with a friend like Austin. Our little creek was my favorite place to fish and play, but I had almost drowned in it. We planted the seeds, and they were washed away by the rainstorm. The tortoise was an ugly, old creature who could hardly move, and yet he challenged the hare, who was fast and sure of himself, to a race. It went on and on. The world was tied together by opposites, and somehow I had to find my way between them.

CHAPTER TWO

WHY WAS GOD'S WORLD SO HARD?

When first my father settled here,
Twas then the frontier line;
The panther's scream, filled night with fear
And bears preyed on the swine.

Sarah was nine and I was seven. It was the time when the elms, the sassafras, and the hickory turned yellow, and the maples streaked the hills with red. It had been cold in July, so it came earlier than most years. Several months before, Papa had left in a wagon with some of our furniture and a load of whiskey, which was currency. He came back a while later, but neither he nor Mama said anything. We just went about what we'd always done.

Finally, Mama came out with it.

"Abe and Sarah," she said, "you knowed that Papa been to Indiany. He says we can git by up there."

Mama must have thought we'd be happy to get on, but I could read in Sarah's face what I was feeling myself. Although we knew about this, we weren't sure it would come so quickly.

"He's been there 'cause we got to leave. If we don't git from here, they'll pitch us off. It's something with the land. They never knowed who owned this place."

"Mama," I asked, "does that mean I got to say goodbye to Austin?"

"I'm 'fraid so, son, and we got to say goodbye to someone else who's resting up there by the tree."

Sarah took it like she took everything else. While I couldn't stop my crying, she stood there like nothing had happened. Mama hugged her, and she started to cry in Mama's arms.

Mama held Sarah and looked over at me.

"Abe, there's something else. Papa says we cain't take Honey. He says that dog is jes' one more mouth to feed."

"What'll we do with him?"

"We'll jes' have to leave him here."

I couldn't talk to her. I couldn't look at her. No one could ever question what Papa said.

I ran to the woods. It was worse because Honey followed me like we were off on another chase.

It turned out that when Papa left before, he took his tools, some of our belongings, and the whiskey barrels and set off for the Ohio River. Before he got there, his flatboat keeled over in the Rolling Fork, and he lost half his load. He made it across the Ohio, and a farmer named Posey helped him cut through the Indiana woods to our new claim.

Then, in December, it was our turn. We took what little we had left—Mama's cooking things, our clothes, and the blankets—and set off. Sarah and Mama were on one horse and Papa and I were on the other. We were all a-shiver. Honey tried to follow, but Papa yelled at him and he slunk away. I couldn't look at him.

We said goodbye to relatives and friends in Elizabethtown and then plodded through the Kentucky fields and forests. Each night we set up camp, and Mama cooked us a sparse dinner. We huddled together by the fire. If it snowed, the flakes hissed down into the fire. We didn't sleep much because the blankets couldn't keep us warm.

Papa said we'd come to the river. I could see we were getting closer from the large cut through the distant trees. We started down into a wide valley. From our valley at home, I could tell what was coming. Sure enough, we went down the slope and into a clearing, and there was the Ohio River.

Although it was gray in the fading December light and although the river was surrounded with brown, leafless trees, it has stuck with me. Rather than rushing rapidly and grandly past us, it was drifting lazily toward the west.

When we arrived at the ferry, we left the horses, carried our possessions aboard, and waited for it to move out into the river. Ever so slowly the ferry started to ease toward the far shore. Everything was so calm that when the men from the stern started to shout, it caused a frightful ruckus.

"What's that coming for us?" one of them yelled.

"Looks jes' like a big coon," said the next.

"That ain't no coon. It's some mongrel set out when it seed us leave."

"It cain't make it, although the current ain't bad."

"Hey, little feller," one of them bellowed, "git along home."

Papa and I joined the other men.

Suddenly Papa shouted, "It's that stinking mongrel that done belonged to Abe."

It was Honey! He must have followed us all that way, sticking to himself and keeping clear of us because he was afraid of Papa.

I didn't think about it. I jumped over the stern and into the freezing river. I could swim better than the time I was almost drowned in the creek, but I figured that if I didn't get Honey fast, we both might go under. I swung my arms through the water and kicked hard toward him. When I got closer, he started barking and howling up a storm. I grabbed his neck and started pulling both of us toward the shore. I was lucky that we weren't that far out.

The ferry was turning around. Whether Honey got the idea or not, I don't know, but he started paddling with me even though I still hung on to his neck. We came closer to the shore, and then I knew we would make it. When we both climbed out onto the bank, he jumped all over me, whining and fussing and licking.

The ferryboat docked, and Papa ran over to Honey and me. I was thinking I'd get the worst beating he could give me with the others watching.

He hovered over us. I was crouching away from him, shielding myself from the blow, but all he did was say, "Abe, I reckon with what you done for that dog, and what that dog done for you, it ain't fair not to let you keep the little feller."

Once we crossed the river, we came to Posey's farm, where Posey loaned Papa a crude sled and a pair of oxen to labor along with us through the Indiana woods. We put all our goods on that sled, and sometimes, when he was tired, Honey climbed aboard.

In those days, Indiana was nothing but thick, deep forest. Some of the oaks and sycamores towered over a hundred feet. In some places, the sun could not get through. There were Indian trails, but the underbrush grew over them very quickly. The first time he went, Papa hacked through the grapevines that popped out of the undergrowth and tied themselves up in a sturdy net between the hickory, beech, and ash trees. It was only sixteen miles from Posey's to our new home, but it was mighty slow going. Sometimes we came to a swamp or a creek bed, and the sled weighed down hard on the oxen. While there weren't any woods in those Bible stories Mama read us, it seemed like God was putting us through one of those trials he gave the people of Israel to see if they'd stay loyal to him.

We didn't say much to each other as Papa walked ahead and we came after. In the morning it was dark, and the woods were close all day. It was sad and gloomy all through. Even our little fire in the evening was cheerless. Although it was cold and raw, we could hear the creatures scratching and scuffling through the sticks and leaves next to where we slept. I wasn't afraid of them, but Papa said that panthers and bears might be nearby.

God may have helped us or we might have made it on our own, but finally we came to the rise where Papa had staked his claim. He'd marked our place with the things he rescued from the flatboat and that Posey helped him get there. This place was called Little Pigeon Creek after the flocks of pigeons that flew over the Indiana woods. It was wild and isolated, but there were six or seven families nearby.

Papa built what was called a half-camp. There wasn't time to build a whole cabin since we would have frozen to death. The half-camp was three walls and the fourth one open to the winter. It was open to the south, the direction from which the storms didn't come. At least that was the idea. Our fire burned in the open space, which warmed us some, but if the wind changed, it blew the smoke into the camp. Mama and Sarah coughed and wheezed most.

Maybe because the winter came early, it loosened up early. Papa showed me how to use the axe. I helped him cut the logs for our new cabin. The neighbors helped us build it like they had in Kentucky. Papa set it up the same as our Knob Creek cabin, although this new one was bigger, and it had a loft at one end where I climbed up to sleep. It had a dirt floor and cracks in the walls, and the fireplace had the chimney on the outside. Where Papa set it was not near the creek like the neighbors, and it was my job to fetch the water.

Papa went back to Posey's to fetch some hogs, and he told me to use the rifle to kill some game for Mama and Sarah. A flock of wild turkeys came near the cabin. I saw them through one of the cracks. Mama loaded the gun for me. I told Mama and Sarah to hush up, put the gun into the crack, and pulled the trigger. The noise alone scared me, and the kick from the gun almost knocked me over. I went out and found one of the turkeys with its head shot off and its blood splattered all over the ground and the trees nearby. It made me sick to see what I had done. Since then, I've never pulled the trigger on any game.

Papa came back with news that he'd seen Uncle Thomas and Aunt Betsy Sparrow. Mama was so happy when he told us that the Sparrows and Dennis Hanks, my eighteen-year-old cousin, were coming to Little

Pigeon Creek in the fall. I was still missing Austin, but I hoped Dennis could take his place.

When they arrived and settled in, Dennis helped me with my reading and writing. Since Dennis was so much older, it was different from being with Austin.

One morning he told me, "Abe, you take them letters you larn'd with Riney, and you fix 'em into words. Where's your mama's Good Book?"

It was on the hearthstone in front of the fireplace. I brought it over to the table where we sat next to each other.

Dennis dug through the pages casually.

"Here's a good 'un," he said, and he started to read haltingly.

"And it came to pass, as soon as he came nigh unto the camp, that he saw the calf, and the dancing: Moses' anger waxed hot. . . ."

Dennis paused and said, "Well ain't that somethin'. He's so mad at them for making that gold calf, he can melt candles. Them Israelites is always doing wrong. Nope, we can't use that one. We got to larn you right."

He fussed a bit, saying there was some stuff about Abraham that I should know.

"It's in the Book of Genesis."

He paged through it back to the beginning.

"Here it is, Abe. It's when God is telling Abraham that he's going to make him a king or something like that."

Dennis read again, "And I will make of thee a great nation, and I will bless thee, and make thy name great; and thou shalt be a blessing."

He continued, "Now them letters can be done different. If you takes *a*, which can be *a* like in *hay* or *a* like in *rat*, then you got *e*, which can be *e* like in *me* or the *e* like in *git*, then you takes this *e* and that *a* and you puts them together like in *great*, as in what I done read you, and you gits a sound like *a* as in *Abe*. You git that, Abe? You jes' has to figger that out from what you is reading. And it's jes' like that when you done your writing. You has to figger out what them letters is doing and spell them words like in the Good Book."

I appreciated what Dennis was trying to do for me, but somehow I figured I'd be better off on my own.

Dennis helped me with some of my chores. Even so, at night I was so tired I could hardly climb the ladder up to the loft. Dennis slept next to me. When he climbed up, the ladder was always squeaking and groaning.

One night we woke to a frightful ruckus. Something was crashing through the bushes, and then it sounded like the rails Papa had put up for the hog pen were being cracked in half. The hogs were grunting. Honey's shrill barking came faster and louder. Then we heard a squealing and a growling together at once. Something was being mauled and smashed to the ground. The cabin was shaking.

"It's a bar," yelled Papa, and he ran to the wall where his gun was sitting on its pegs. Dennis and I hopped down the ladder as fast as we could. Mama and Sarah were up from their bed. Papa ripped open the door, and we rushed outside. It was too late. In the moonlight, we could see a trail of blood flowing toward the smashed-up brush.

After looking around the pen and counting up the hogs, all Papa said was, "He git one, but tomorrow we'll git him."

In the morning, Papa and Dennis got set for the bear hunt. They wanted me to come. I didn't mind the tracking, but even though the bear stole from us, I didn't want to be there when Papa and Dennis brought him down.

"Abe," Papa said, "this ain't no time for mercy. Them hogs is our food, and I'm fixing to sell most of 'em this fall, even that little one you been trying to make a pet of. We got to protect us from that bar."

"What good will it do to kill him, Papa?" I said. "Another one'll be coming after the hogs. You cain't kill all the bears in this forest."

"No, Abe," said Dennis with a smile, "when them other ones find out what happened to this one, they ain't coming around here no more."

Papa and Dennis set out on their horses. They carried their rifles and were accompanied by Honey and Fido, a mongrel puppy that Posey gave us. The dogs picked up the scent in the clearing by our cabin and plunged into the brush. They followed the trail of smashed vines and saplings that the bear made when it lumbered through the woods toward the hog pen by the side of our cabin.

The dogs yelped when they found the remains of the bear's half-munched meal. There was the evidence all right: the hog carcass with its innards spilled all over the ground. When Papa and Dennis caught up on their horses, the dogs rushed ahead. They heard more high-pitched barks, and they knew the dogs were back on the trail. Over logs and creeks the horses charged, and as Dennis's horse bucked over a large tree trunk, it threw him into the brush. Dennis got right back on, and it wasn't long before he was up to Papa and the dogs.

When they'd gone on for a way, they spotted a black shape moving through the trees. They were surprised to see it outrunning the dogs. Once or twice the bear turned around, foam and drool dripping from his hanging tongue. Before long the dogs circled the bear and had him at bay. Dennis and Papa caught up and fired at him several times.

With its eyes afire, the bear reared up and tore at the dogs. They shot at him again and again. Blood was spurting from his head, his chest, and his limbs, but he kept fighting like he didn't notice. Finally, with a loud bellow, he fell forward and collapsed on the ground.

Papa and Dennis argued about who'd get the bearskin because it belonged to the person who killed it. As they went at it, the two dogs jumped onto the hulking corpse and claimed the skin for themselves.

I told Papa and Dennis that neither of them should get the bearskin. They should give it to Mama, who was always freezing in the winter. When we got back, I rushed to find Mama, but she was over with Aunt Betsy and Uncle Thomas.

They were living in Papa's half-camp for the winter. Aunt Betsy and Uncle Thomas had been like parents to Mama and grandparents for me. We were a bigger family, and with Dennis and me taking on more chores,

Papa could do more of his carpentry work. I thought that like Moses, we had come through our trials.

Then the sickness came.

The first one was Mrs. Brooner. When Mama visited her, she told Mama she was dying. Mama told her not to worry herself and that she would soon get better. Mama seemed to know about this, and it wasn't until I heard her talking to Papa that I knew differently.

Mama told him that Mrs. Brooner was a sight to behold. The main thing was the pain. She was thrashing around, vomiting, and moaning in her bed all night and day. She was in and out of convulsions, her breathing was fast, and her eyes rolled up into her head. Her tongue was getting bigger and had turned all purplish-red. It went on for almost a week. Finally, her heart was beating too fast. Mama told Papa she was in a coma. That meant she would die soon. There was no doctor for thirty-five miles, but he probably couldn't do much for her anyhow.

It was the milk-sick. The cows were dying at the same time as the people. We didn't know the cows were connected to what was happening. Somehow their milk was infected, and the disease killed them too. If we had known this, we could have come through it.

But we didn't.

Then Aunt Betsy and Uncle Thomas took sick. They came down with it at the same time. Even though Mrs. Brooner had died, we didn't think it would happen to them. From what Mama had said about Mrs. Brooner, it just didn't seem as bad, but Mama told us to keep praying for them.

I found places to walk through the woods in this Little Pigeon Creek area. It was as pretty as Kentucky. Mama was always saying we should take comfort from the Bible, but that didn't help me much with seeing Aunt Betsy and Uncle Thomas get sick. Mama seemed so much happier with them around. I asked God not to take them from us.

But after the first days, it turned worse. Mama nursed them and knew what was coming. The sadness was written deeper and deeper into her face. Papa turned away from her and just kept chopping trees and carving boards from the wood. They didn't talk when we were together for supper, and Sarah and I didn't say much to them.

After Aunt Betsy and Uncle Thomas died, it was like the life went out of Mama too. When she came down with it, she had nothing left. She had the trembles, which was the first sign. We hoped it might be something else, but then it was just like all the others. She was convulsing in her bed with pain in her stomach and crying for God to help her. She would sometimes be herself but most times not. It was so hard to see Mama like that. Somehow the only way we could think about it was this must have been what God set up for her.

Papa sat by her, but mostly he stood by the door looking out at the woods. It was October, and there were things he had to get ready for winter. When Papa was outside, Sarah and I would sit with Mama and keep ahold of her hands.

She held on for a week, and then she called us to her side.

"Abe and Sarah," she whispered slowly, "God is taking me. Be good and kind to your papa."

Her words came in short gasps.

"Remember what the Book says and what I done tried to teach you. Be good to each other and to the world. Love and worship God."

Later that night she fell into a coma and was dead the next morning.

For the next two days, Mama's body lay on her bed in the cabin. We ate and slept near her. Some of me wanted to sit next to her and just look at her face, which was peaceful, and some of me wanted her to rest in the ground—mostly when the flies found her and she started to smell.

Papa had built the coffins for the deceased, and I helped him build one for Mama. The oxen pulled it up on a large board to the place where we had buried Aunt Betsy and Uncle Thomas. Papa dug the hole in the ground where Mama could rest. Papa, Dennis, and I lowered the box into the grave, and Papa shoveled the earth back on top of it. We laid wildflowers on the dirt. The trees were bright shades of red, yellow, light brown, and green. Papa had chosen such a pretty place for Mama, Aunt Betsy, and Uncle Thomas that it made me even sadder. There was no one to bless Mama until later when Preacher Elkins came up from Kentucky.

Each of us took it in our own way. Papa just went about as he had before. He didn't talk much, and he and Dennis went off hunting most days. By now Sarah was eleven, and she took on most of what Mama had done. When I was off in the woods with Honey, I just put my arms around him and cried.

After the crying passed, the deep sadness came over me. Like the fog, it lifted when the warmth and brightness of the world returned, but if they receded, it settled back into its familiar place. I could hear Mama's voice when I read the stories from the Bible. I could see her smiling at me in Sarah's face and when Sarah looked up from mending my clothes. I could smell and taste her in the rabbit stews that Sarah cooked for us. I could feel her placing the blanket over me as I crept into bed.

Sarah tried to stand in for Mama. She did her best, but it wasn't the same. It was hard being the only woman with Papa, Dennis, and me. Some time after Mama died, I came into the cabin and saw her crying by the fireplace. I put my arm around her shoulders just as she had done so many times for me.

"Abe," she asked, "why did Mama have to leave us?"

"It weren't up to her," I said quietly.

"I know that, Abe, but why was God taking her when we needed her so?"

"That's just his ways, Sary. Least that's what Mama told us."

"Oh, Abe, I know," she said, "but it just don't seem right. It just come so quick."

"Do you pray for her every night, Sary?"

"Of course, Abe, that's what she told us to do."

"Well, I do too, but there is some nights I cain't."

—◦—

In the time after Mama's passing, it was a hard winter and a cool spring. Dennis and Papa hunted but they didn't bring back much. I helped clear some more of the brush and trees, but it was too soon to use the land for planting. Because he was so low after Mama died, Papa stuck to himself and didn't talk much. He just needed Sarah to fix his meals and me to do my chores. He was with Dennis more since they were off hunting so much.

Papa took a load of hogs through the forest and down the river for selling. He wanted to get away for a bit. When Papa left, things were even sadder. Mama had held us together, and Sarah couldn't keep up. She was best at cooking but not at the spinning and mending or cleaning. Our clothes were tattered and torn—we didn't wash them much—and the cabin was messy and dirty.

Papa came back, but he didn't seem to notice or care. In the summer and into the fall, our crops were poor. It was the weather and the soil. The hunting was lean, so we didn't have much food. When things were bleakest, Papa up and left again. He said he was going back to Kentucky and might be gone longer this time.

———

Why was God's world so hard? Just when we were getting started in our new place, just when we were coming together as a family, we were stricken with the milk-sick. Mama had cared for the dying. Why did she have to die herself? If there was one thing I could never imagine, it was our lives without Mama. She had held us together and now she had been taken from us. Even if Papa and I could help, the load was too heavy for Sarah.

What would happen to us?

When I went for my walks in the forest with Honey, the world seemed a place of shadows. I wept for Mama. Honey seemed to know how I felt. He stayed close and rubbed his head against me when I stopped and looked down at the ground.

It was being with Honey that helped me begin to understand. We had abandoned him, but that didn't keep him from believing in us. He followed his family for seventy miles. He was willing to swim the Ohio River to be with us. He taught me what it meant to be determined, to be faithful to a purpose. Mama was right about those people in the Bible. They didn't understand God's ways, but they kept believing in His goodness.

CHAPTER THREE

YOUR NEW MAMA

Near twenty years have passed away
Since here I bid farewell
To woods and fields, and scenes of play,
And playmates loved so well.

Papa left in the fall, and when the winter came and he didn't return, we thought we might not see him again. He'd said he was going to visit relatives, but we hadn't heard from anyone. We were surviving, but things were mighty bleak. I cut the wood for our fires, Dennis killed just enough game to keep us from starving, and Sarah cooked what we had tolerably well. We had all lost weight and probably looked like wraiths. We had little to do with the neighbors who used to stop by just after Mama died. The snowstorms kept us more apart than ever.

Near the time of my birthday in February, there were some days when it thawed up, and the trail from the river was passable. Although there were ice chunks on the river, it never froze over. Sarah had been sick and was resting inside, but Honey and I were out looking for Dennis.

From far away, I thought I heard oxen plodding along the trail. Was that two riders on a horse ahead of them? Was that three more riders on a horse behind them? I thought these must be ghosts from my imagination.

They were not.

It was Papa and a boy riding on the same horse, and a tall woman with two girls on a horse behind him. The oxen were pulling a sled that carried a large load under a cover.

The woman called out to Papa, "Tommy, this must be Abe. Look at how tall he's gotten."

She climbed down from her horse and helped the girls to dismount. Papa and the boy stood near her.

She reached out to give me a hug, but I held back.

"Now, Abe, is that the way to treat your new mama?" she called to me kindly.

"Abe," said Papa, "while I was away, I done married Mrs. Sarah Bush Johnston of Elizabethtown. We was known to each other formerly. You and Sarah now has a new brother, John D., and two sisters, Elizabeth and Matilda."

Mrs. Sarah Bush Johnston was as tall as Mama, but she had much lighter skin. She was pretty, and her eyes lit up when she smiled. She wanted to know all about Sarah and me.

Papa took her and our new brother and sisters into the cabin so that they could meet Sarah. When Mrs. Johnston walked in, the smile and the gentleness left her face.

"Tommy, how could you let these children live like this?" she said angrily. "Why, if I had known about this, I might not have joined up with you."

She stroked her hands through my hair, and then turned toward Papa. "Why, Tommy, Abe's head is full of lice, and Sarah looks like the wind could blow her over, poor dear."

Mrs. Sarah Bush Johnston changed things. She was different from Mama and Papa.

People in Elizabethtown lived simply, but Mrs. Johnston was more of a lady than anyone in Mama or Papa's family. She liked things clean and neat, and she cared about the clothes she wore. She wanted us to look better than when she first came. Before long, Sarah and

I were wearing some of the things she brought up from Kentucky. She hadn't been much to school, but she brought some books with her, and she spoke clearly and used the proper words. She was warm and kind to Sarah and me.

"Abe and Sarah," she said, "I don't want you to call me 'Mama.' You must always remember your mama, and it isn't right for you to call me by her name. You call me 'Sally,' and John D., Elizabeth, and Matilda will call your papa 'Tommy.' That's the way it will be."

When she first came, she soaped us up and cleaned off all the dirt we had on us from over a year. Honey got a bath too since she said he smelled something awful.

The first thing she had Papa do was put a wood floor in the cabin. Dennis, Papa, and I cut the logs and shaped them so they fit together. Then she said there would be windows and a proper door, and the table and the stools would be sold. Papa didn't spark back at her, probably because he knew she was right.

She brought nice furniture, even though Papa wanted her to sell it before they left Kentucky. It fit in just as she wanted. We had a new table for eating, and there were chairs to go with it. She brought her own spinning wheel and replaced the run-down one that Mama had used. There were chests and other pieces with drawers, and there were two beds that wouldn't have to stick out from the walls. The place was so gussied up, it wasn't near the same.

Where there had been just the five and then four of us, there were now eight people in that cozy space. All the children were from ten to thirteen, and all of us got along just fine. Things started to set up with Papa taking a like to John D. and Sally taking a like to me, and the girls and Dennis got along just fine.

Sally was so open and friendly with the neighbors that we visited back and forth. They wanted to see how Sally had changed things, and they were anxious to meet all the new family. More families were coming in to Little Pigeon Creek, and we got to know them all pretty quick.

It was because of Sally that I began to read so often. She told me to use any of the books she brought with her. I looked them over on the shelf that Papa built for her. In the middle of them was that one called *Robinson Crusoe*. Sure enough, it was about a man who lived on an island by himself for years.

I was able to work myself all the way through, and I found out more interesting things than why Robinson Crusoe called his friend Friday. In the very first pages, Robinson lives in England, and he is torn up about his wanting to go to sea after his father says no. I was so interested in this that I started to write down passages on paper and then on a board if there was no paper. Once I got going on this, I started to write them in a copybook.

I still remember this one from *Robinson Crusoe*. Robinson is thinking to himself:

> I resolv'd not to think of going abroad any more but to settle at home according to my father's desire. But alas! a few days wore it all off; and in short, to prevent any of my father's farther importunities, in a few weeks after, I resolv'd to run quite away from him.

He has a few shipwrecks, ends up on the island, and
believes God is punishing him for defying his father.
At first it sounds like Jonah, but Robinson thinks he's
more like Job. He prays to God to forgive him, and he
thinks in the end that God rewards him. It was strange
in those books of Sally's how much everything fit in with
the Bible. Robinson's disobeying his father sounded a
bit like what I heard in church about us being sinners
for disobeying God. There were also places where
Robinson's island sounded like the Garden.

I also found out why Robinson called his friend
Friday. It's because Robinson saves Friday, and the day he
saved him was a Friday. I wrote Austin to tell him why he
was wrong, but Austin never sent back.

I read all Sally's books and then got some more from
the neighbors. My favorites were *Aesop's Fables*, *Pilgrim's
Progress*, the *Life of George Washington* by Mr. Weems,
The Arabian Nights, and *History of the United States* by Mr.
Grimshaw. I loved to read books. I was finding out about
things that were different from our life in Indiana.

It was Mr. Weems's book that first excited me about
our country. George Washington's struggle at Trenton,
the crossing of the river, and the fight with the Hessians
fixed in my mind. I couldn't understand it all, but I
wanted to know what kept them going. Mr. Weems said it
was the words from the Declaration.

When I was thirteen, Sally leaned on Papa to let us
go to Mr. Crawford's school. It was another of those blab
schools. It ran from the harvest time until we could start
planting again in the spring. The schoolhouse was a run-

down cabin with benches that had no backs on them but plenty of splinters. Bugs and spiders were everywhere. Mr. Crawford made us memorize and recite our lessons, and sometimes he whipped someone for misspelling a word. Because it was so noisy from everyone saying their lessons, I started to read aloud to myself. I have done it ever since. It helps me to understand what I am reading from both seeing it and hearing it. Aside from my siblings, Nathaniel Grigsby and Anna Roby were my best friends.

One Friday afternoon, Mr. Crawford was picking the words for our spelling test from his copy of *Webster's American Spelling Book*. Maybe he was trying to find out how hard to make the words, but he surprised us by yelling out, "Allen Gentry, spell the word squirrel."

Allen looked up at him and didn't know what to think. He asked Mr. Crawford to say the word again. He probably had trouble hearing it, since John D. was sitting next to him saying letters from his spelling lesson, and I was on the other side of him reading aloud to myself.

"C-h-i-p-m-o-n-k," blabbed out John D., covering up a word in his own book. Then he looked at it and went, "Nope, that ain't it."

"Once the wolves sent an embassy to the sheep to make a peace treaty between them for the future," I read from Mr. Crawford's copy of *Aesop's Fables*.

"Gentry," said Mr. Crawford angrily, "spell *squirrel* . . . spell it."

"S-q-w-i," said Allen. "No . . . that ain't right."

"C-h-i-p-m-u-n-k," said John D. "There, I got it!"

"'Why should we continue such deadly strife?' the wolves asked."

"Gentry!" roared Mr. Crawford. "One last chance . . . *squirrel.*"

"S-q-w-i . . . Oh, Mr. Crawford, I cain't do this with Abe and John D. makin' such a racket."

Mr. Crawford shushed everybody and then gave us the spelling test. When we finished, he looked over the papers and scowled at us.

"I should whip each one of you," he said, "but none of you will go home for day or night until one of you spells this word . . . *defied.*"

"D-e-i-f-y-e-d," yelled out Nathaniel Grigsby.

Mr. Crawford said nothing.

"D-e-e-f-y-e-d," said John D.

"No," said Mr. Crawford.

"D-e-i-f-i-e-d," tried Elizabeth.

He didn't blink.

"D-e-f-y-e-d," whispered Anna Roby.

Mr. Crawford was beginning to realize that his plan had gone wrong. If we had to stay here for day and night, so did he.

While he looked away in disgust, Anna looked over at me. I put my finger up to my eye.

"D-e-f-i-e-d," she called out confidently.

I didn't ever cheat, but if we could outfox our teacher, somehow that didn't count.

Up to the time I was fifteen or so, I worked for Papa mostly on our land. Dennis and I chopped down trees and cut them into firewood. It was my job to cut up the tangles of underbrush, while Dennis hacked away on the stumps. Sometimes we dug them out together. It was tough work, and we slept pretty well when we finished a day of it. When the trees were down and the stumps were gone and the underbrush cleared out, we could work the land. Papa would plow it with the oxen, and Dennis and I would hack away the clods with hoes. We did all this in the spring to get it ready for the planting.

Once it was planted and growing, then came the weeding. Dennis and Papa left that to me when they went off hunting. It took a while to figure out which were the plants and which were the weeds, but I caught on. Papa would let me do it in the morning and again in the late afternoon, which was nice because it was so hot. At the end of the summer came the harvesting. I had to help with digging the potatoes and picking and shucking the corn.

I would always have a book by when I was working, and sometimes, when we eased up from what we were doing, I would open it and start reading. Papa would yell at me and ask what I meant by it. Was I trying to be better than him? I didn't say anything, but every chance I got, I still did it. I heard him arguing with Sally about it, and she took my side.

There were the hogs, the oxen, the horse, and some chickens to be fed, and that was my job too. Papa sold most of the hogs down by the river, but he kept some for us to eat. When he said he was going to be slaughtering, Honey and I took off for the woods. One day, Papa told me I had growed up and I couldn't hide from it no more. He taught me how to do it. I never got to like it, but I could do it.

Papa was always on the short end with money, but about this time he was in even more trouble because of a loan. He decided he could pay it back if he pulled me out of school and hired me out to the neighbors. I did most of the jobs for them that I had done for Papa—chopping down trees, clearing the land, making fences, daubing their cabins, and slaughtering their hogs. Papa took all the money I earned. Somehow I didn't mind so much at first, since most of the neighbors let me read while I was working for them. And it was the chance to talk to men other than Papa and Dennis.

It was when I was working for Mr. Crawford that I got myself into some trouble. This was a different Mr. Crawford from the schoolteacher. He knew I was reading while I was doing the work. It was from him that I got Mr. Ramsay's book about George Washington. I learned most of it by heart.

Some time after, Sally gave me a look to frighten the devil.

"Abe," she said, "that book you borrowed from Mr. Crawford is ruined."

"What?" I exclaimed. "Now, how can that be?"

"You left it up there in the loft, and the rain came in through that leak that Dennis was supposed to fix. The book is wet through and the pages are stuck to each other. It's completely ruined."

She seemed both angry and sad.

I took the book over to Mr. Crawford and told him how sad I was that I had ruined his book. I told him exactly what had happened.

He said, "Abe, this will teach you a lesson. I don't want the book back. You will keep it, but you will pay for it."

I said, "Mr. Crawford, I've got no money. My father takes it all. What can I do?"

"You'll work for me until the book is paid for."

He put me to work on his farm picking and shucking the corn. He pushed me hard. By the time I was finished, I could have bought four copies of that book.

Papa and Sally went to church every Sunday. Sometimes I went and sometimes I didn't. I went to see my friends, and I liked it when the preacher got himself worked up. I didn't go for that kind of religion, so I was thinking about how I could make fun of him. I enjoyed entertaining my friends, and they laughed most when I mimicked people they knew.

One time, when we'd all been to church the previous day, I was at home chopping wood for Papa. Allen, Anna, Nathaniel, and the others were there, and they said, "Abe, you can clown real good. Let's see you do the preacher."

I jumped up on a stump, started to wave my hands and arms in the air, and yelled like I was talking to a big crowd, "Why, when the Judgment Day comes to all of you, the Lord will come down and separate the sheep from the goats. You just remember that the Lord was a shepherd and that he wanted all of us to be his sheep. He said he'd give up all the good sheep just to rescue the one that was lost. But if you don't obey his word, it ain't no good to be a good sheep or a lost sheep. You'll just be one of them goats."

Nathaniel jumped up and said, "Preacher man, how does I know if I done be saved?"

"Brother Nathaniel," I called out, "you will know when you feels the sweetness of the Lord. It's real sweet. It comes to you in the morning when you says your prayers, it stays with you for the temptations and tribulations of the day, and when the sun sets and the darkness moves over the land, it comforts you from your sorrows. It's real sweet."

They were all rolling and poking each other from laughter, and I was enjoying it more than they were.

I guess Papa didn't think it was so funny, because he broke it up by telling me I had to get back to work.

It was one thing to be funny, but I regret to say that I also did something that was mean. It happened when I got together with my friends. John D. and I would sneak out of the cabin at night to join up with Allen and Nathaniel for a coon hunt. I never liked hunting, but it was something for us to do. There was one problem.

When John D. and I got out the door, Papa's little yellow coon hound barked at us like to wake up the whole cabin.

"Joe," we whispered. "Here, Joe, come along with us."

He shut up and bounded along with Honey and the rest of us.

It was dark, but we could see just enough through the trees for us to follow where the dogs were taking us. Pretty soon they scented a coon and began to holler. Finally, we came to a tree stump where they had the thing trapped. Allen was the first one there and he shot it quick and simple. Although there was blood dripping out from the holes in its head and neck, most of the rest of it had no blood on it.

"Hey," said Nathaniel, "I got an idea. We'll skin this critter, and then we'll take the hide and tie it over old Joe. Maybe that will keep him from telling on our coon hunts."

We all agreed that this was just the thing, and we began to work it up. Allen skinned the coon, I held down old Joe, and John D. tied the hide together around him. Old Joe was growling and fighting us the whole way, but we got it done. When we finished, he ran off like a shot to get back to Papa.

Without us knowing this would happen, the other dogs around our farms got wind of Joe, but they thought he was a coon. They ran him down near our cabin and tore him to pieces.

The next morning Papa came out and found some of the bloody pieces of Old Joe. He figured out in a jiffy what we had done to him.

John D. and I stood in the doorway.

Papa came over to us and said, "I kin think of what I done as a boy, but none of it ain't close to this. John D., this ain't what I'd think you'd ever do, and Abe, ain't you the one that stops the boys from burning the turtles out

53

of their shells? Ain't you the one that's said an ant's life is precious to it? You done saved that hound of yours, and you done something like this? Git on back, both of you. I don't like starting the day with a licking, but I got to learn you for this."

We took our whipping, which was one of the worst Papa ever gave me.

What happened to Joe wasn't right. I couldn't think why I had done it. The only thing I could say for us was that we didn't intend it to end that way.

When I was seventeen, I had a job that took me away from the farm. When we first came to Indiana, we crossed over the river and landed at Anderson's Creek. It was where hogs and corn were shipped down the river, and Papa knew Mr. Taylor, who hired young men to work his ferryboat. Mr. Taylor paid me six dollars a month plus a place to stay.

I had never seen such people as those who rode the ferryboat across the river. There were preachers, politicians, pioneers, and people talking out against slavery. There were trappers going out west to trade with the Indians, teachers looking to find a town with a schoolhouse, gamblers, and people talking for slavery. They all talked to me and asked me about Indiana. For some it might be right, but most said they would probably move on.

Anderson's Creek was where the river turned lazy and still. Sometimes at night I would sit on the bank and listen to the voices coming up from the town. The reflections of the moon and the bright stars glittered across the water. One night a steamboat with its lights aglow bustled along, and I said to myself, "I got to get down this river someday."

I started thinking about how I'd liked being away from Papa, and the way it was so easy to talk with the people I'd met on the ferryboat, but I also thought how much I liked being alone, just sitting there and looking up at those stars. I had listened to those preachers, but I couldn't make much sense of what they said. It was all a mystery, but one I wasn't sure I'd ever understand.

I was thankful that Sally had come into our lives. She encouraged me to read, and it was through reading that my world was expanding. She convinced Papa to send me to Mr. Crawford's school, but it was Papa who removed me so my wages could go to him. I felt the first stirrings of anger toward him. Sally tried to intervene, but there was no getting around Papa when he was set.

Papa was right about my growing toward being a man. I was nearly six foot tall, and because of doing Papa's work, I was getting stronger. I could whip all the pups around Little Pigeon Creek in any contest with an axe or lifting things. I was also pretty fast when I ran races, and I was the best at wrestling. I didn't pick a fight, but I could take care of myself when I was in one.

I didn't like what I saw coming, but I knew I would start bucking Papa. Why was he so angry when I was reading? Why couldn't he let me learn at school? Why couldn't he let me make fun of the preacher? He was just too set in his ways and wasn't going to let me find my own.

CHAPTER FOUR

There Was More Out There

As leaving some grand waterfall,
We, lingering, list its roar—
So memory will hallow all
We've known, but know no more.

I got my chance to go down the river.

James Gentry, Allen's father, owned a store in Gentryville, a little over a mile from our farm. Mr. Gentry got rich from trading hogs and corn down in New Orleans. He'd hire men to float his cargo down the Ohio and Mississippi Rivers on a flatboat.

When I was nineteen, Mr. Gentry hired me to help Allen build a flatboat and then take it downriver. We'd trade and sell the supplies and then break up the flatboat and sell it for wood. After staying a few days in Orleans, we'd come back by steamboat. I was itching to get out, since I'd never been anywhere but the backwoods of Kentucky and Indiana. Allen had been there before, so I went along as the hired man.

Allen and I chopped the trees, cut them into beams, girders, streamers, and planks, and fit them all together. I had carpentry skills I learned from Papa, and they came in useful. The flatboats were eighty feet long and eighteen feet wide, but since ours was a two-man boat, it was half as long and not as wide. All the flatboats had a storage space with a roof over it, maybe a half of the length. It was the place to keep the load, and it gave Allen and me shelter. Where we slept, there was a wood stove for heat and cooking.

For steering, Allen stood on the roof and used a long oar. I was at the bow with a shorter oar, which I used to guide us in the current. It was also my job to look out for the sandbars. If we got stuck on one, we might not get off and the flatboat could go over. Everyone said we should be down and back again in two months. Allen was now married to Anna Roby, and just before we left, he knew Anna was expecting their first baby.

We planned to leave with the hogs, corn, potatoes, and flour in early October. It rained so much the summer before that the river was flooding over its banks. Flatboats could float at four to five miles, so this meant we'd be going faster. It also meant the dangers would come faster, and we'd have less time to react. The high water would carry us over some of the sandbars, but it could also hide other dangers.

In early October, we set off from Rockport near Anderson's Creek. We moved out into the river and steered the flatboat toward the current. We eased ahead and rounded the first bend. Anderson's Creek receded into the distance and then it was gone. It was as if my first years were behind me. I was at the front of the boat, and the open water, the virgin forests, the circling birds, and the limitless sky were all calling me forward.

We floated during the day, and we figured we'd make between thirty and forty miles. Some flatboats went day and night, but our crew was two and we had to sleep. Since Allen had done it once, he pointed out what we were passing. On the Ohio, it was all forests up to the banks like we cut through when we went to Indiana. It was fall and the leaves were beginning to turn. At first the tips of the trees were yellow and red, but as we floated southwest, the colors brightened. There'd be cows and sheep and villages on the bank, but most of the settlements were small. Sometimes people waved and asked where we were going. We passed cliffs and rocks mixed in with the forests.

We were on the Ohio five days.

Allen pointed something out to me. He looked over at the north bank, the one on the right, and he said, "Abe, all the people up here on this side is free," and then he motioned to the other side on the left and said, "Not all the people on this side is free. This is where they have the slaves." Most of the people from Little Pigeon Creek were against slavery. Papa said his church didn't think slavery was right. I never thought about it much, but it did seem strange to have it one way on one side of the river and another way on the other.

Pretty soon we came to the place where the Ohio flowed into the Mississippi. Allen knew about this, and he warned that if we didn't take it right, we could lose the boat and the cargo. I had never seen such a powerful rush. There were cross rips and whirlpools that could take us under or turn us around quick. The water levels were different in the two rivers, and that scrambled us around. Allen was steering and yelling at me to put my oar to the right or the left. We shot out halfway, and then the current from the two rivers together swept us down south. We were on our way to New Orleans.

For the first miles, we could see that the waters had not mixed together yet. The water from the Ohio flowed pure and clean next to the muddier waters of the Mississippi. As the waters finally joined together, we were on a different river. This one meandered more than the Ohio. There were so many bends that it was taking us twice what it would on land. The valley for this river was lower and wider than the Ohio.

For the next two weeks, we settled in quite comfortably. Most of it was just floating down the river, but we were watchful. The river gave us warning if we read the signs. I got better at seeing them. I could tell when we were coming close to a sandbar or if there was a downed tree just under the surface. We could get snagged or it could punch a hole through the side and sink us. There were some storms, and they made steering and staying in the channel pretty tough. Most days we began at dawn and floated until the twilight. If we went a little farther, we had the stars and the moon for company.

When we set in for the night and tied her up, sometimes another flatboat would pass on down. Some of those flatboats had larger crews, and they'd be playing music or dancing to pass the time. We recognized the songs and joined right in as they went by. There was a bond among the people going down the river.

One night, Allen and I caught some catfish and cooked them up for dinner. We lay around by the stove swapping stories and jokes. He was telling me how sweet it was to be married to Anna and that I should get myself a girl.

"Nope," I said, "I ain't so sure what's coming next for me, so it don't make sense to get saddled."

"Abe," says he, "ain't you goin' to settle and git a farm of your own in Gentryville?"

"I ain't sure, Allen. It's what Papa wants, but it ain't what I want."

We passed down to a place Dennis had told me about. It was when he was back in Kentucky and he was a boy of twelve. He just remembered one day that the ground started trembling and then he almost fell over. He always called it "the Shaking of Earth." Whenever he talked about his days in Kentucky, this was the first thing he'd say. I reckon it really scared him. I'd always heard people saying something about it, but no one like Dennis.

When we came there, we could see that the banks were lower and the trees were leaning over. We stopped at a town called New Madrid, and they told us about the December '11 quake and how they thought it was the end of the world.

We passed the place they were starting to call Memphis. It wasn't much, but further down in Louisiana, there was a big place on the Mississippi side called Natchez, where we stayed for the night. There was a fleet of flatboats tied up in the harbor by Natchez.

When we drifted deeper into Louisiana, we began to trade some of our hogs and corn for sugar and cotton that we would sell in Orleans. There was lively trading going on at the plantations with most of the flatboats. Below Baton Rouge was where we had the trouble.

When we were done for the day and finished with supper, we leaned up against the side of the flatboat next to the fire and swapped some more stories.

I thought I heard rustling on the front part of the boat.

"Did you hear something, Allen?"

"I did, Abe, but I don't hear it no more."

We went back to laughing and joking.

When I heard it a second time, I told Allen I was

going to get up and look around. I walked past where the roof stopped and the deck ran forward. It was toward the bow where I poled all day. It sounded like someone had climbed aboard. Although the fire from the stove gave off a glow, I couldn't see much in the dark.

What came next was so sudden, I didn't know at first what was loose.

Three men jumped at me with clubs and swung them wildly. Most of them missed, but one of them caught me hard near my right ear. I could feel the blood streaming out and running down my neck into my shirt.

I yelled at Allen for help. He came quickly with an axe handle and swung back at them. We were able to hold them off, until they were joined by more attackers.

"It's a gang of them," I cried.

Allen went down with a bad gash on the left side of his face. Blood spilled out onto the deck.

"They're going to kill us," he cried out.

We were overwhelmed. There were seven of them. We could see they were Negroes, maybe slaves from the plantation near where we tied up. They were trying to rob us, but they would murder us first if they had to.

All that work I had done for Papa and the neighbors had strengthened and toughened me. When Allen fell, I moved in. They couldn't all jump me at once. Two or three of them went down, and then Allen was back up beating them with his handle.

They were yelling at each other to come at us from the side, and then we were surrounded by the five that weren't down. I heard a crack and a scream and saw that one of them got Allen in the ribs. My shoulder hurt so much it was probably broken. It didn't look like we could hang on. They had figured out there was no one nearby to help us.

Allen was always good when things turned quick. I was too, but I didn't come up with the plan that saved us.

He yelled at me so loud that they all could hear.

"Lincoln, get the guns and shoot."

When they heard this, they bolted over the side. They weren't going to tangle with us if we could shoot them. They cut out so fast that Allen and I were left on the deck bleeding and staggering before we fell down.

We crawled back under the roof and collapsed by the stove. I realized Allen had scared them off by bluffing. We didn't have any guns aboard.

We were hurting pretty badly. We hadn't been on the river much at night, but we had to get out of there. We moved out fast and had a good run. With the first light, it was clearer going. Allen said we should make it to Orleans by sunset. My head hurt, but my shoulder just ached, which meant it probably wasn't broken. Allen felt the same, but his ribs hurt him something bad.

That day, while I was up front poling by myself, I was thinking about why those Negroes almost killed us for what we had on board. I couldn't make any sense of it.

It had been a beauty of a day and the sun was sinking far off. We rounded a lazy bend, and there was the city of New Orleans. There she blew! That's what those whaling men would say. And we felt the same way they must have.

The last of the sun caught the roofs, the church steeples, and a large white-gray dome. The masts and sails from the ships stretched across the harbor. There was smoke coming from boats and from round columns on the shore.

When we drifted into the harbor, Allen knew where he wanted to go. There was a wharf just for flatboats. There must have been almost two hundred of them. When we docked, it was like an anthill. There were the flatboat pilots like Allen and the flatboat hired hands like me. Most of them were carrying the cargo onto the dock. There was a separate place to lead the livestock. There were agents for the companies that wanted to buy the flatboats' cargo, and among them were some plantation men in fancy dress. Some flatboats brought cargo that had already been purchased. Since nobody had bought ours, we had to find the men who would bargain for it.

From the docks rose the first smells of the city. There was food cooking in the houses close to the water, there was the smell of the livestock, there was the smoke from the steamboats and from the flatboat stoves, and mixed in was the stench from outhouses. That same stench was coming from the water.

For the next couple of days, we lived on the flatboat and sold our supplies. We got good money for the hogs but less for the corn, the sugar, and the cotton. We met Mr. Gentry's expectations, so we had done our job. Next was tearing down the flatboat and selling the wood. New Orleans consumed wood like a feral beast. We got a good price for it, and then we were on our own for a little bit.

I had never been near anything like Orleans. There were French, Spanish, Indians, Negroes, and people they called Creoles. The Creoles were mostly French, but also a mix of Negro and either French or Spanish. They had their own language, which was also a mixture. We stayed in a run-down boardinghouse that was near the bars and the places with women. It was pretty rowdy. The flatboat men didn't have a good name. The people who lived there said all we were interested in was drinking, gambling, women, and fighting. Allen and I kept clear of all that. We didn't drink much and we wanted to keep hold of our money. Allen was newly married, and we'd already had our piece of the fighting. We ate at the boardinghouse and had mostly fish and rice. The coffee was the best I'd ever had.

The streets were paved with stones that were once the ballast for the ships. I'd never seen so many people. We had to be careful when we walked anywhere. Negroes were driving horses and mules through the streets, and they were pulling carts that rocked all over. There were light posts for the night, which meant it was never dark in the city. People were always around during the day or night. It was the first time I'd seen slavery up close. I'd mostly read about it in the newspapers.

Back in Indiana, whenever I could, I started to read the newspapers. The one I liked most was the *Louisville Courier*. There were always local things, everything from lawsuits to who was getting married, but also national events. I perked up at those. It may have come from reading about George Washington or Grimshaw's history.

I wanted to know more about what was going on in the country.

In Orleans there were newspapers in English, Spanish, and French. I'd never seen so many. The ones I read were talking about the election in the fall between President Adams and Andrew Jackson. Jackson had almost won the election before, and he kept saying that Adams and Henry Clay had kept him from winning. Now he was running again, and the newspapers said he would probably win. I was starting to learn about the political parties and trying to find out more about them.

I saw notices in those newspapers in Orleans about slaves who had run away and for slave auctions. If those slaves who beat us back up the river were runaways, we didn't think too highly of them. Allen and I wondered about the auctions, but we didn't go because we had to get on back. Most of the Negroes we saw in Orleans went about their business and kept to themselves. Some were free, but the only way we could tell was they were dressed a little smarter.

We returned by steamboat. The newspapers talked about how the steamboats were unsafe because their boilers sometimes blew. There were fires, and people were burned and drowned. Allen and I had seen a burned-out steamboat on our way down the river, but that didn't keep us from going back on one.

When we came down the river, it was just us, and most of the day we were poling on our own. When we went back up on the steamboat, there was a crowd. We talked about our trip coming down and our time in

Orleans. The other folks had stories that were as much fun to hear as the stories we told them. It was quite something to be on that boat. We took two months to come downriver on the flatboat and just two weeks to go back upriver to Indiana.

Allen was jumpy to see Anna and to feel if her belly had swelled some. I was mixed about going back. Being on the river and in Orleans had shown me what was outside Indiana, and I knew I'd be itching to get away. I was feeling strange. If those slaves had no chance to be free, I didn't either. I'd be doing work again for Papa and the neighbors and giving him all the money. I'd found people who told stories about things I'd never seen or done. The newspapers opened my mind to a wider world than Gentryville. There was more out there, and it was working away on me.

CHAPTER FIVE

I'VE BEEN A SLAVE IN THE FREE STATES

Abraham Lincoln
his hand and his pen
he will be good but
God knows when.

"Abe, how much did you git from old man Gentry?"
"After he paid us for the steamboat passage, it was twenty-four dollars, Papa."

"Ain't no more than that?"

"Nope, Papa."

"Well, that'll come in handy. It's been hard since you been gone. The spring was cold and we ain't planted half of what we should. The hogs ain't throwed and when they do it won't be much. It's been three years now since we git what we need."

"Are you going to take it all?" I asked.

"Yup," he said, "I ain't got no choice."

"When do I get a parcel of it, Papa?"

"Abe, you ain't got no complaining to do around here. Whatever you git comes to me. You've knowed that."

"But, Papa, I've growed up. Ain't it time for me to get just something? Allen got to keep most of what his papa gave him."

"Abe, you might have growed bigger, but you ain't got no right to that money."

"What does Sally say?"

"Abe, you git me rising on this if you don't lay off."

"It ain't fair and it ain't right."

"Where'd you git that? From those newspapers you been reading all day long? From those books I seen you with when you is supposed to be working? From hanging around with ole Brackenridge and Jones? The neighbors is talking about they ain't gitting a full day's work from Abe Lincoln because he's reading or making fun of the parson. They say you got notions that come from that trip to Orleans. That's costing me what's coming in from you."

"I do want to see what's beyond here."

"Abe, I been to Orleans doing what you done. That done it for me. I git back to Kaintucky and stick with what I always done. You ain't got no reason to do much else."

"I don't want to do what you've done. It ain't for me."

"Abe, it ain't up to you. For all I done for you, the law says you are bound to me. You do as I says, you do your chores, and you git me that money."

"Sheriff Turnham and Mr. Brackenridge say I am free at twenty-one."

"So they've been gitting you them notions. Well, that may be what they think the law says, but I ain't raised you to run off from your papa. You stick around here, git a gal, and work your own farm, and you'll do what I done."

Papa was right. I had been talking to Colonel Jones, Lawyer Brackenridge, and also Sheriff Turnham.

From Sheriff Turnham I got a book that surprised even Sally.

"What do you want with that old dry thing?" she asked.

It was the *Revised Statutes of Indiana*. In it were all the laws of Indiana. It might have been dry to most, but to me it made a kind of sense that I didn't get from any other book. All the laws fit together and told people how to live with each other. If we could do that, we'd all get along better. I also liked how the laws were written. The words kind of sang together in my head.

Also in the *Revised Statutes of Indiana* were the
Declaration of Independence, the US Constitution, and
the Act of Virginia. The Declaration jumped out at me. It
was the words and the thoughts. In our new country, all of
us had the right to live, to be free, and to follow our own
ambition.

Colonel Jones owned the store in Gentryville. It was
a place I could go to swap stories and talk politics. He
got the Louisville newspaper every week, and there was
the news of the national election. Papa was for Andrew
Jackson and the Democrats, but Colonel Jones was
for Henry Clay, who made more sense to me. Henry
Clay was from Kentucky, and he wanted national
improvements like roads and canals. He was in favor of a
national bank so that our money would all be the same.
The farmers wanted Jackson, but Colonel Jones and
Lawyer Brackenridge went for Adams and Clay.

Lawyer Brackenridge invited me to see him in court.
I liked how the court was run. There was a way of doing
things that everyone agreed to. The judge was in charge,
but since it all rolled out like a clock ran, he didn't have
to do much. The jury sat quietly and listened to the
lawyers and the witnesses. Things went back and forth
between the two sides, and the lawyers made it hard to
see who was right. Lawyer Brackenridge had me come to
a murder trial where he was the prosecutor. I skipped off
from my work and hoped that Papa wouldn't find out, but
I couldn't miss it. On the last day, Lawyer Brackenridge
gave his talk to the jury, and it was clear and powerful.
After the jury ruled for him, I told him I'd never heard

anything like his words to the jury. He said it looked like I belonged in the courtroom and that I'd be a lawyer someday.

That sure wasn't going to happen if I stayed in Gentryville.

If I was itching to get away, Sarah wasn't. She was so pretty and sweet that we knew it wouldn't be long before someone noticed. Aaron Grigsby took a shine to Sarah, and she sure liked him too. The Grigsbys were the high class in Gentryville. In 1826, when she was nineteen, she and Aaron were married. Aaron built her a cabin, and they lived near his family.

I missed Sarah something bad. We'd been through everything, and she was the one who kept us together when Mama passed and Papa took off for Kentucky. She was kind and sweet and just wanted to make everyone happy. Aaron was lucky to have her.

While Papa was hiring me out for the money he got from my work, we heard that Sarah was going to have a child. We were all so happy for her. No one would be a better mama. We could see her swelling, and she always had this look of everything being just fine. Sally visited her every day to help her through.

Soon it was her time to deliver. Sally told us that she was starting to cry out with the pains. For some women, mostly with the first one, it could go on for a while. Papa, Dennis, John D., and I were working on our farm and waiting for the news.

Sally came back in the afternoon looking weak and pale. We all gathered in the cabin to hear what was happening. She told us that Sarah was screaming more than usual and that the women with her were scared. The Grigsbys sent for the doctor, but the word came back that he was drunk and gone to bed. They couldn't rouse him. That night could be the worst of it.

Just before dawn, we heard a knock on the door. Papa opened it and let in Nathaniel. He couldn't hold back the tears. Sarah was gone, and the baby girl was born dead. No one said anything.

For days, I didn't talk to anyone. I just sat down on a log and let the tears roll down my face. First Mama and now Sarah. Sarah was always so gentle, and she was always looking out for me and for us all. None of the sorrows I read about in the Bible or any of my other books were like this. They were no help. I said to myself, "I have nothing left to live for."

It was true. I could barely force myself to do the farm work, and it was all I could think about. Sometimes I found that the work helped me with my anger at Papa, but not with Sarah's death. I just couldn't get over the sadness. It was with me all the day and night. Sally tried to help, but I couldn't listen.

"Abe, it hurts us all so deep. You don't have to take it any harder than the rest of us. Sometimes it seems that you have all our sorrows on your back."

I couldn't say anything to her in return. I just left the cabin and walked endlessly through the woods. At night when I couldn't sleep, I'd go outside and look up at the stars. If I had ever thought it was a good world we lived in, I couldn't think that any more. Why did Sarah pass so young? Sally said God had taken Mama and Sarah and they were now with him. She said it was Adam's sin that caused all this. I was tired of trying to explain it with stories. My mind was awakening, and I wanted to live by what I could touch and know. All l knew was sadness. All I could touch faded and died. The grief and mourning passed, and the sadness drew back a little, but I knew that it would always be with me.

When Papa got over his grief, he started to feel the anger. It knotted up in me as well. Papa wasn't sure that the Grigsbys had done everything they could to save Sarah. Why hadn't they tried to find another doctor? Why hadn't the women done something when they first knew things weren't right? What about these women? If they hadn't been able to help Sarah, were there some others who could have? Maybe the Grigsbys thought Sarah wasn't good enough for Aaron. They had always looked down on us. When Papa had thoughts like this, they churned away in him.

He decided to have it out with old man Grigsby. If there was ever someone cantankerous, it was Grigsby. Papa and he started small, but before long they were yelling at each other back and forth. At least that's what Papa told us. He said it went on for a while and stopped just short of fisticuffs. There was no chance of those two ever speaking to each other again. There had never been bad blood in Gentryville, but there was after that.

Everyone in Gentryville except us was invited to a double wedding for Reuben and Charles Grigsby to Elizabeth Ray and Matilda Hawkins. Papa was furious, but I got back at them another way.

You see, I had taken to writing poetry—what Sally called doggerel. Some of it was above that, but this called for a piece of real doggerel.

I made it sound like the Bible and called it "The Chronicles of Reuben." It was full of all sorts of "And it came to pass . . ." phrases. I made it up that there was a double wedding feast with everything to eat and drink and lots of dancing. Then everyone went home and it was time for the grooms and brides to go to bed. The grooms were so drunk they didn't know which end was up.

Now, there were two bedrooms upstairs, one on each side of the hallway. When it was time for the grooms to go upstairs, the mother, who was also drunk, got confused and sent them to the wrong rooms. After a bit, she figured it out and sprang upstairs to tell Reuben that he was in bed with Charles's wife. Well, it all broke loose after that.

I copied this out several times, kept it anonymous, and left it where people in Gentryville could find it.

Reuben challenged me to a fight, but I told him I'd lick him easily. Instead Reuben agreed to fight John D., who said he was game. There was a huge crowd because the word got out. John D. and Reuben swapped hard punches, but pretty soon Reuben got the best of it. John D. went down and looked like he wasn't going to get up. He was hurt pretty bad. I broke through the crowd, grabbed Reuben, and threw him as far as I could.

At this point I couldn't resist. I stood tall and yelled, "I am the big buck of the lick!"

This was too much for the Grigsbys and all those who

were on their side. They'd been drinking heavily all day and wanted to finish off John D. and pummel me. They swarmed over us like hornets, piling on and grabbing and punching. If they could hold us down, I knew that the kicking and biting would start. We'd be lucky to escape with a bloody beating.

Fortunately, there were enough people who hated the Grigsbys that they came in on our side. With rallying cries, they pulled off the Grigsbys and their friends one by one. Ears were yanked and torn, teeth knocked out, and foreheads split.

I was able to protect John D. and myself. We worked our way out of the brawl, and although beaten and bruised, we were able to limp home.

After several days, I had recovered and was reading in the cabin when Sally came in and said, "Your papa says he's going to give you another whipping."

I was ready for it this time, so I just said, "Sally, you've been a mama to me, but you can't stop what's happening between me and Papa."

"Abe, I've seen it coming. It eats at me."

"He can't keep me here."

"I know that, Abe."

Papa charged through the door saying he'd been looking for me most of the day. He had a hickory switch in his hand.

"You git outside. I don't care if it's raining. You got this coming."

I stood up and glared at him.

"You got this coming. Is you the one that writ that

thing about Reuben? About how he and Charles gone to bed with the wrong women?"

"Yes, I did."

"That's what they says. You stirred 'em up like hornets."

"You were just as angry at them as I was. You had it out with old man Grigsby. It was my way of getting back at them."

"That's what they says. You did it 'nonymus, huh? How was you thinking they wouldn't know?"

"I didn't care. I don't care now."

"Well, you gonna care when I'm done with you. You come out here and take what you got coming to you."

"You ain't going to lay a hand on me."

"So you is now the big buck of the lick. That's what comes of all this eddication you been gitting. I told Sally it weren't no good. Reading when you was supposed to be working so we could eat."

"Yes, I've been reading about something called tyranny."

"Oh, so your pappy, who is just asking what is due him by the law, ain't as good as you 'cause he cain't read."

"When Allen and I were going down the river, he said one side was free and the other was slave. I've been a slave in the free states."

"You ain't no slave. Sally and your mama and I been agin' it all our lives. It ain't right by our religion. You ain't got no religion so you ain't got no business going against me for making you a slave. You ain't no slave."

"You take all I earn. I got a place to live and food to

eat. That's what they give those slaves."

"After I done with you, you git back up to Crawford's and clear that place back of his barn."

"You ain't coming near me."

He made a move toward me and Sally sprang in between us.

"There ain't no blood between father and son in this house," she cried.

That was it.

I stepped away. If he'd tried to whip me, I would have fought him off. He looked at me with hatred and with hurt. He hated me for what I wanted to become—more than an itinerant carpenter. He hurt because he did not understand me. He had never tried and it came to this. The bond between a father and his son was torn for good and he knew it.

By the *Revised Statutes of Indiana*, he was right. I was bound to him until I was twenty-one. If he wanted to make me his slave, I had no choice. I learned later there was something people called the "letter of the law" and the "spirit of the law." By applying the letter of the law, he lost me as a son. I would serve out my time and then, like Robinson Crusoe, I would depart from my father and never see him again. He would be gone from my life.

Two years later, Papa decided that he'd had enough of Indiana. The farm had never been much, and the sickness that killed Mama and the Sparrows was back. Dennis was now married to Elizabeth, and Tilda had matched up with Squire Hall. Cousin John Hanks, who'd lived with us a bit, moved to Illinois and sent back saying it was ripe for farming. Papa sold the farm, and we all lit out for Illinois.

It wasn't easy, but we settled in near the Sangamon River by Decatur. It was just like Indiana when we first got there, except this was the prairie. It wasn't woods to cut through, but we'd have to plow up the deep-rooted grass before anything could grow.

I helped build the cabin, plow up the fields, and plant and harvest the crops. There was time for me to hire out, and I did that mostly by splitting rails.

We settled in for the winter, but this was colder with more snow than we'd ever seen. After a blizzard in December came even more and more snow. Most days that winter there was four feet of it. It was brutally cold, and the cattle and horses died when their feed ran low. There was no going out to the fields to get more for them. It went on for weeks.

When spring finally came, Papa decided to move to Coles County.

I did not go with him.

Cousin John Hanks had tied up with a man called Offutt who wanted three men to be the crew of a flatboat he was taking down to Orleans. Cousin John, John D., and I set out in canoes for Springfield to meet up with Offutt. By the *Revised Statutes of Indiana*, I had attained the age of majority.

I was heading out on my own.

PART TWO

New Salem

Chapter Six

A Piece of Floating Driftwood

Where many were, but few remain
Of old familiar things;
But seeing them, to mind again
The lost and absent brings.

"Pole left," I yelled to him.

John D. was in the front section of the flatboat on the port side. The river was up after the melting of the deep snow, and we were moving quickly. He pushed his pole down into the rushing brown water. It rippled as the pole entered and left whirlpools when he withdrew it.

On this sunny May morning, the violets and dandelions dotted the hillsides with purples and brilliant yellows; in the distance, the emerging leaves of the hickories and elms were a delicate yellow-green. Kingfishers swooped over the river with their rattling cries.

We steadied in the current and moved to the middle of the river. Cousin John Hanks was starboard opposite John D., I was atop the front of the overhang, and Offutt was sitting below me eating an apple. The river was not wide, so it was not difficult to find the channel.

Ahead was a bend to the right. Again, John D. poled hard on the port side, and I steered us into the turn with my long pole. As we rounded it, with the stern of the boat sweeping toward the left bank, I saw a nest of log houses up over the hillside on the left. Smoke from the chimneys floated eastward toward the river. The pounding of iron upon iron echoed from a blacksmith's shop. Men were carrying sacks of grain or corn down the hill. Directly ahead, stretched out into the river, was the framed structure of a mill. Near it, small children scrambled on the riverbank.

On the far side, a large gray-backed bird stood several feet out into the river. With its brownish-yellow bill slightly open, it arched its neck toward the water. Everything about it was rumpled, particularly the black plumes extending from the back of its white head.

As we drew closer we could see the grist and saw mill propped on wooden pilings that were filled with rock. We heard the grinding of the millstones and the raspy pitch of the saw. Merry shrieks came from the children as they played a game of fox and goose.

The large bird seemed uninterested in the activity around the mill or the cries of the children until it spied a boy slowly sneaking toward it. It turned its head and followed his slightest movement. Before the boy could cock his right arm and release the flat stone he had been rubbing in his hand, the bird stretched its wings. It flailed awkwardly at the air and ever so gradually powered itself into flight. Its wings began to beat rhythmically and it rose gracefully into the sky. I watched it ease away upriver, which caused me to make a serious mistake.

Because the runoff had swelled the river, I could not imagine we would not skim across the rocks of the milldam and be on our way to Beardstown. If I had been more alert to what could happen, I might have been able to prevent it.

"Pole right," I called out to Cousin John Hanks. "We'll go over the dam to the right of the mill."

The bow slid forward and began to scrape over the rocks in the pilings. Then, as the flatboat wedged further along, the scraping became a deep grinding growl. The bow of the flatboat was suspended several feet in the air, while the stern, submerged in the river, began taking on water.

The children were delighted by this. They rushed up the hillside toward the town, crying, "Flatboat's stuck on the milldam. Everyone come down and watch it sink."

"We'll have to get the boat unloaded or it will go under," I yelled to the others.

Offutt jumped off the flatboat and searched for the village on the hillside with a dreamy, abstracted look.

"Offutt!" I yelled at him. "You okay with us unloading the stock and supplies?"

Offutt did not answer.

I had to take over.

Imprisoned in their pen, the hogs were squealing. Barrels of corn and pork were now immersed in the water we were taking on. We had to get this cargo off our boat. If we did that, we could balance the flatboat on the top of the dam.

"Let's unload those barrels onto the shore, and shift the others to the bow. Then we can get the hogs. That ferryboat is coming over here. Looks like they can take the rest."

We were joined by volunteers from the village. Most of the residents were happy to have an excuse to drop their chores on a lovely spring morning.

"Onstot's boy come up and told us you were in a fix," said a tall, muscular man.

"Thanks, fellas," I said. "If you could pitch in and help us with the barrels and them hogs, we'd be obliged."

Together we were able to get the hogs to the shore and to move most of the barrels to the ferryboat. We couldn't have done it without the help of our new friends.

Now the problem became the large volume of water that had swept into the boat and anchored it down on the dam.

"What will we do?" moaned Offutt.

"Abe'll think of something," replied Cousin John.

I appreciated the confidence, but I could do nothing except ask the people on the shore if they had any ideas. No one did.

While we sat together on the riverbank, we introduced ourselves and learned that most of them were men with trades. Helping us were the blacksmith, the cooper, the tanner, and the owner of the tavern. We told them we were on our way to New Orleans to sell Offutt's livestock and supplies. They told us their village, New Salem, was just getting started. They hoped that traffic on the river would help it to grow. Before long we were swapping stories and yarns. Still, no one could figure out what to do about our flatboat, which at least wasn't sinking anymore.

Somehow the plight of our flatboat made me think of Aesop's fable about the fox and the boar.

A fox met a boar who was sharpening his tusks on a tree. "Why are you doing that when no hunter is near?" asked the fox.

The boar replied, "If danger overtakes me, I won't have time to sharpen them, but they will be ready for use."

Here we were in danger, but without any tusks.

Wait, I thought, that's it!

"Has anyone got an auger?" I called out to the men on the shore.

"What would you do with that?" asked Mentor Graham, the schoolteacher.

"You'll see."

"Onstot the cooper . . . Henry's got one," spoke up Jack Kelso.

Henry Onstot stepped forward. "William, go up to the store and fetch my auger for young Mr. Lincoln."

Onstot's shop where he made his barrels was at the other end of the village. While Billy ran to fetch the auger, I whittled a wooden plug from a tree branch I had retrieved from the river.

I could hear one of the Rutledge girls ask, "What's he doing that for?"

"Not sure," replied Mentor Graham.

Billy returned with the auger and gave it to me. I stepped back into the flatboat, walked forward, and started to drill an inch-wide hole into the bow.

"Ah, now I see," said Graham, "this young man has a fine head on his shoulders. He knows exactly what he's doing."

When the bit of the auger pierced through the boat, I climbed out. John D. and Cousin John tilted it up, and the water rushed forward and started to gush out of the hole. It took an hour for the water to empty from the boat.

When the water had drained, I plugged the hole with the wooden cork I had fashioned earlier. We pushed the stern of the flatboat and maneuvered it over the dam with surprising ease.

Offutt climbed down the bank and stepped into the shallow water. He forgave my faulty navigating and congratulated me on rescuing the flatboat and his cargo.

"If it weren't for you," he said, "I would have lost everything. Abe, this town's got a future. They'll be sending steamboats up this river to Springfield. If I were to build a store here when we get back from Orleans, would you come and manage it for me?"

"I would," I replied.

—•—

This time we had an easy passage down the rivers to Orleans. Offutt's cargo and the flatboat fetched a good price, and after a few days there, he sprang for steamboat tickets back to Illinois.

Cousin John and I returned to his family near Decatur, and I stayed with them. After a few weeks, it was time for me to head out for New Salem.

I hoped it wasn't for nothing. Was Offutt reliable? I wasn't sure.

When he'd rounded up John D., Cousin John, and me for the trip to Orleans, he said he'd have the flatboat ready for us by mid-March. We got to Springfield and couldn't find him. Next day we came across him, dead drunk, in a tavern. He hardly recognized us and muttered something about why there was no boat. It took us six weeks, but we built a flatboat for him.

Maybe Offutt's plan to build a store in New Salem was all gas, but his offer to clerk there and manage it was the chance I needed to get out on my own. I hadn't done much and didn't own a thing, but I wasn't going back to Papa and Sally.

I figured I could canoe on the Sangamon River from Cousin John's to New Salem. It was fifty miles. It might take two days, but I'd done as much as that before. For part of the way I'd be following the same route we'd been on three months before when we'd taken Offutt's flatboat to Orleans. I'd be coming into New Salem from the southeast.

On a burning hot July day, I set out.

Most of my life I'd been by myself. I sure loved company, and nothing beat making them laugh, but I was fine just being by myself. I got to like having my thoughts come up one at a time and then mixing together. Sometimes if there was a sad one, I set it aside. Most of the time that worked just fine.

The heat and humidity were oppressive. No clouds and no rain had brought day after day of wilting sunshine. Even the hours near dawn or before dark brought no relief from the heat. It was not the time to be active.

Although the heavy, soupy air hovered over the river, it was cooler than walking the prairie trails in the stifling heat. Occasionally I drifted under some sheltering trees by the riverbank. There was variety in the twists and turns the river had carved out for itself.

Every now and then a fish would leap up and then plop back, leaving ripples on the surface. As I canoed down the river, my thoughts streamed in and out just like the eddying pools my paddle made as I lazily stroked the brownish-green water.

I was on my own at last, but I was little more than a piece of floating driftwood.

Paddle right . . . paddle left . . . into the current.

I remembered the words Mama had often read

from the Bible. "In the sweat of thy face shalt thou eat bread, till thou return unto the ground; for out of it wast thou taken: for dust thou art, and unto dust shalt thou return."

Stroke left . . . bow to the right.

I knew one thing. I would not spend my life earning my wages "in the sweat of my face."

It was my reading that changed me. I owed that to Sally.

But hadn't I read that Robinson Crusoe sinned by disobeying his father and going to sea?

I would never stop reading and studying.

Stroke right . . . bow to the left.

"Good boys who to their books apply will make great men by and by." I wrote that in Joe Richardson's copybook back in Indiana.

Why would I write something like that?

Ripples ahead . . . go around the snag.

I had left my father. Would I be punished for it?

How would the people of New Salem see me? For the strange, uneducated, penniless boy that I was?

When I arrived at New Salem, Offutt was not there. I can't say this was unexpected, given our prior experience with him. There was news that he had obtained his license to open the store a few days earlier and that he had purchased a lot near the mill.

James Rutledge invited me to board at his tavern if I would help with some of the seasonal work. My first job was to cut the wood for the tavern's fireplaces and to transport it from the woods nearby. Most of the settlers had cut down the trees on their plots and owned pieces of timberland on the outskirts of the woods. We used horses or oxen to drag it back to the village.

The town was established by Mr. Cameron and Mr. Rutledge in 1828. They were looking for a place to build a mill and a dam, and they found it on this northern bend of the Sangamon River. The land on top of the hillside was flat and offered a good place for the village, just as Cameron and Rutledge had hoped. Farmers came from all around to grind their corn and grain, pioneers and tradesmen settled in New Salem, and the river trade started to pump up the economy. Before long the town was home to a cooper, a cobbler, a wheelwright, a blacksmith, a hatter, a tanner, a shoemaker, two doctors, and several shopkeepers. Some of the families came from New England, and others, like me, migrated from Kentucky. Isaac Gollaher, Austin's older brother, journeyed there from Indiana.

The people in New Salem remembered me as the young man who saved the flatboat, and they welcomed me to the village. Some of them said that I must have grown six inches in two months since my pantaloons were halfway up my calves. It wasn't the first time people had made fun of me for being so tall or how I dressed.

One of the advantages of living at the tavern was that Mr. Rutledge's daughters were pretty. I'd been around girls before, but they always felt like sisters.

Back in Indiana one night, Anna Roby had pressed up next to me while we were on the banks of the Ohio and said, "Look, Abe, the moon is going down."

"That's not so," I said. "It don't really go down. It seems so. The Earth turns from west to east and the revolution of the Earth carries us under, as it were. We do the sinking, as you call it. The moon as to us is comparatively still. The moon is sinking only in appearance."

Then she had said, "Abe, what a fool you are."

I took a real shine to one of the Rutledge girls. This was the first time I had strong feelings for any young woman, but I heard she was already engaged, and that was the end of it.

Even though I had just arrived, I decided to vote in the election on August 1. The voting was conducted on the front porch of James Cameron's house. I stepped on the wooden planks, approached the trestle table where the judges and the clerks were sitting, and told the judge the name of my choice for Congress.

"Edward Coles," I said loudly.

He was the candidate favored by Henry Clay. I found out later that most of the people in New Salem were Democrats and therefore went for Andy Jackson's choice. The judge called out my name and the name of my candidate. It was recorded by the clerks.

Then came my vote for justices of the peace.

"Edmund Greer and Bowling Green."

I had already met Bowling Green, and I'd heard that Greer was fine too.

"For constables?"

"Jack Armstrong and Henry Sinco," I replied.

One of the clerks was my new friend, Mentor Graham. He asked me, "Abe, can you write?"

"I can make a few rabbit scratches," I replied.

"Can you help me keeping these rolls?"

"Sure can," I said.

Mentor put me right to work. When I voted first thing in the morning, the line stretched almost to the Rutledge tavern, but by afternoon it let up. With no one around, the judges and the clerks started to swap yarns.

From the first day when I was down by the riverbank waiting for the water to flush out of the boat, they'd already learned I liked telling stories.

Mentor turned to me and said, "Got an election yarn for us, Abe?"

"Well, I might."

"Let's hear it then, Abe," called out Jack Kelso, who was also clerking.

I started with a flat, serious tone.

"On election day in Kentucky where I'm from, it rained before the voting, and the roads were muddy. There was a drunk in town whose name was Bill.

"Well, Bill tied one on and laid himself in the mud where he slept all day. In the afternoon, he recovered and started for the pump to wash himself before voting."

I stumbled slightly to imitate Bill's gait on his way toward the town. I half closed my eyes, scrunched my face, and muttered to myself, mimicking his condition.

"When he reached the town, another drunken man was leaning over a horse post. Bill mistook the drunk for the pump and used the man's arm for a handle, which set the occupant to throwing up.

"Bill put his hands under and gave himself a thorough washing.

"When he got to the polling place, the clerk looked at him and cried, 'Why, Bill, what in the world?'

"Bill replied, 'You should have seen me before I was washed.'"

I finished with a look of wonder on my face to resemble what Bill's expression must have been.

Mentor roared and slapped his thighs, and Jack rollicked around a bit.

"Abe, you sure got . . . the knack . . . for tellin' a story," sputtered Jack, while he tried to control his laughter.

———

In late August, Offutt finally arrived. He had plans to build his store on the eastern bluff just above the river, and he negotiated an agreement with Cameron and Rutledge to operate the mill. He'd also hired another clerk, Bill Greene, who lived with his family near New Salem. Bill's job was to figure who could and who couldn't pay the bills. There was plenty for both of us to do.

The design of the store was simple. It would be a small log house with a front door and no windows in any of the side walls. A fireplace in the far end would give warmth and some light in the winter. There would be shelves all around to store and display the wares.

It would have an inviting front porch. Offutt thought farmers from nearby would pass the time while Bill and I ground their corn or grain at the mill below. He imagined lively conversations with himself at the center of them. Surely these men would trade their bags of meal and grain for the household goods sold in his store.

It fell to Bill and me to build the store. I remembered what Papa had taught me about being a carpenter, and since both Bill and I had helped other families build their homes, we were able to get it up in no time.

Bill was a handsome fellow. A shrewd look was often on his face. His hair was reddish brown and he wore a beard, which was lighter than his hair. He was shorter than me, and he hadn't used his hands as much, but he learned fast, and we liked working together. He'd been to school and his mind was quick. Bill was known in New Salem for his pleasant ways, and we became friends from the start.

One hot, sunny August day, we took a break, and Bill pointed to the small, run-down log house just to the north of us. It was pushed back almost into the woods.

Bill leaned on his axe handle and said, "That's Bill Clary's grocery. It gets that name because he sells liquor by the drink. It's also where the Clary's Grove boys hang out. They're a rough crowd."

"Why do you call them that?" I asked.

"They get drunk and fight everybody from here and other places all around. They even fight among themselves. Gander pulls are what they like best. That's where they put grease on the gander's neck and tie it to a tree branch by its feet. Whoever can pull its head off while riding past on his horse gets to keep the bird.

"They've had dog fights and cock fights up here. Last summer they found Jordan so drunk he couldn't stand up. They put him in a barrel and rolled him down the hill so that he splashed into the river. If Jack Armstrong hadn't pulled him out, he might have drowned."

I asked Bill to explain something I'd heard in the tavern the night before.

"Row Herndon tried to tell us about Babbs McNabb's rooster, but Kelso said he didn't get it right," I said.

"I was there when it happened," Bill replied. He glowed with the chance to tell the story.

"Babbs got himself a choice fighter from Springfield and challenged the Clary's Grove boys to put up any cock against his. Those were fighting words to the boys. The day was named and the cock pit was set up right over there."

As he said this, Bill pointed to the hollow between the two stores.

"There was betting all around, after which Babbs and Jack threw the two cocks into the pit. Babbs's bird took one look at his challenger, ran around a few times, and then jumped out of the pit.

"Babbs grabbed the bird and flung it out onto a woodpile."

Bill mimicked Babbs's mighty throw with glee.

"The bird squawked angrily, and then Babbs screamed at it, 'Yes, you little cuss of a bird. You are great on dress parade, but not worth a damn in a fight.'"

"Cock fighting and gander pulls," I mused. "So that's why they sold Offutt the land on this side of the town?"

"Yep, they weren't sure about him, and Offutt hadn't figured it out himself. He thought being near the mill would be an advantage."

"Which is a problem since now he is on the same side of the town as the Clary's Grove boys," I said.

When the store was finished, Offutt found Bill Clary poking around one afternoon. Offutt was a short, pudgy man. Since he'd come to New Salem, he'd already gotten the reputation of being a windbag. Bill Clary was stocky, but sturdy. His face was grizzled, and he was a man of few words.

Offutt came up to Bill Clary's chin. They strutted around each other like a pair of roosters ready to fight in the pit between their stores. There wasn't anything those two wouldn't bet on.

Offutt taunted Clary, "My man Abe Lincoln can whup any man in this town. I'll put ten dollars on him. You pick any of them Clary's Grove boys, and Abe'll lick him easy."

"That's the easiest ten dollars ever come my way," returned Clary. "Wait till you take a gander at Jack Armstrong. Your man'll be on his butt faster 'n a rabbit can skitter into them bushes."

From inside our store, Bill and I heard this conversation. Although I had told Offutt I liked to wrestle, he had no idea if I could stand up to Jack Armstrong. I had never wrestled with ten dollars on my head. He did this without asking me.

I was angry at Offutt and ready to tell him I wouldn't do it, but Bill said, "Nope, can't do that. If you don't wrestle, Offutt will lose his bet, and people around here won't like that. They'll want to see Jack whip you, and they'll want to see Offutt cover their bets as well. He's gotten you into a sorry mess. Have you met Jack yet?"

I paused and looked toward the hollow where the wrestling match would probably be held. I said, "I've seen him around, but I haven't met him yet. Mentor told me to vote for him as constable."

"So you've actually seen him?"

"I have."

Jack was short, stocky, and massive. His chest was shaped like one of Henry Onstot's barrels, and his legs were as thick as the wooden pilings on the milldam.

Bill continued, "The only person to ever beat him was Ferguson. Sam Hill put him up to it because he'd had a spat with Jack. Sam was too small to take him on himself so he offered Ferguson some china plates from his store. Ferguson won because he was bigger, but he took such a licking, he always said he'd paid Sam double for those plates."

"No one could beat me in Indiana," I responded.

"I've seen him wrestle. Most of them he finishes off in under a minute. He'd make quick hash of me, but let me show you some of his moves," offered Bill.

We walked over to the hollow between the stores and took the Indian hug position where I set my chin into Bill's collarbone and he did the same to me. We then wrapped our arms around each other. He showed me how Jack would try to get in under my arms and get me close so he could work me over with his vast bulk and strength. Bill also warned me that Jack had been known to bend what few rules there were.

The next Saturday morning, all of New Salem
turned out for the wrestling match. It was held just where
we thought, in the space between the two stores on the
rough side of town.

Since it was early fall, the air was clear and crisp. The
cooler temperatures had driven out the summer heat and
damp. Streaks of yellow and red-orange tipped the leaves
of maple and ash.

The crowd was packed in and already liquored up.
Offutt was taking side bets and the Clary's Grove boys
were finishing up their wagering.

The strong, deep voice of James Rutledge rolled over
the rowdy crowd.

"The boys for this morning's wrastle are Jack
Armstrong and Abe Lincoln."

There was loud cheering for Jack and a few yells
for me.

"The boys will be in the side holt Indian hug. There'll
be no tusslin' and scufflin'—no woolin' and pullin'. First
one that throws the other is the winner. On all bets, I
make the call."

Rutledge paused briefly, and then he yelled at us,
"Boys, get in position."

We stepped warily toward each other on the
trampled grass. We both wore light-colored cotton shirts
and blue denim pants, and both of us were barefoot.

All the years of chopping, scything, and plowing had
built up my muscles. My thighs were plenty sturdy. People
told me later I looked lithe as a panther, but they didn't
think I could hold Jack in a contest of strength.

Jack looked like a large black bear prowling through the prairie forest, and a stirred-up one at that. He eyed me with contempt.

We wrapped ourselves around each other in the Indian hug style.

Rutledge circled around us to see that no one had an advantage, moved back, and then barked, "Wrastle!"

My own neck, arm, back, and leg muscles tensed, and I could feel the same in him. We both grunted as we strained our bodies. There were cries of "Throw him, Jack!" from the crowd.

What the crowd saw was not what it expected. The effect of force matched against force, of strength pitted against strength, was that nothing whatsoever was happening. I had lifted what some people thought was a thousand pounds, but I'd never felt anything like this.

We were stretching our muscles beyond any limit that either of us had known, but neither of us could budge the other. We were joined in a dance of deadlock. The cries of "Get him, Jack!" became more intense as the bettors suddenly realized this was an even contest.

I could feel him shifting to gain any possible advantage on me, but I easily countered any of his attempted thrusts. I was holding out, but I could not begin to think of making a move myself. To do so would invite a deadly countermove. It was now a question of stamina. Which of us could last the longest?

The straining and groaning continued.

Bill told me later that it was Bill Clary who yelled out the instruction for Jack. Clary must have realized that the longer this match continued, the more likely it was that I could win.

Through the haze in my mind and the cheers and taunts of the crowd, I was sure I heard it.

"Leg him, Jack."

Jack seemed to have sensed exactly what Bill Clary was thinking. He might well be in over his head. He took his left arm from my back, grabbed me under the right thigh just above the knee, and with ease, threw me onto the ground.

The crowd burst into wild cheers and hurrahs. They surrounded their hero and held him up on their shoulders. They clapped each other on the back and tossed their hats into the air. The drunken revelry and the shouting continued for several minutes.

I knew what had happened. Jack had cheated. I didn't think about what I would do. I just did it.

When Jack was back on the ground, I walked over to him and shook his hand. He greeted me with equal warmth.

Offutt was quivering by the side of his store. He seemed utterly befuddled and looked over to me for protection.

The bettors, led by Bill Clary, surrounded him and demanded that he pay up. He must have owed them over two hundred dollars.

I pushed my way through the crowd and stood by Offutt.

Then I yelled out at them, "Anyone who wants to collect from Offutt will have to fight me first. I'll take you on one at a time."

The crowd angrily pushed me up against the wall of Offutt's store until a deep, strong voice issued a clarion call.

"This bout was a draw. No money will change hands," bellowed James Rutledge.

Some weeks later I realized that the wrestling match was my initiation into the town of New Salem. These settlers had already proved they had the physical and mental toughness to survive on the furthest edge of the frontier, and they were asking the same of me. By wrestling Jack Armstrong to a draw, I showed that I belonged with them—to everyone from Mr. Rutledge and Mr. Cameron to the Clary's Grove boys. This was the place where I wanted to be, a place where I could settle and learn and grow.

CHAPTER SEVEN

THE CONFIDENCE TO GROW ON HIS OWN

O Memory! thou midway world
Twixt earth and paradise,
Where things decayed and loved ones lost
In dreamy shadows rise.

"How did you get the name Mentor?" I asked Mentor Graham.

We were at the kitchen table in Graham's brick house, which was a quarter mile west of New Salem.

Mentor earned his living as a schoolteacher, but he also made bricks and worked as a mason. He and his wife, Sarah, had built a brick house to remind them of Kentucky, where they'd come from. It took Mentor two years to build the house with bricks from his own kiln. They had the pinkish tint that Sarah liked.

It was late October and the sun was setting earlier than when I first arrived in July. We were beginning to wear woolen shirts. Flames were still licking an oak log that Mentor had put on the fire an hour before.

A single candle burned on the kitchen table. Mentor had a thoughtful expression on his long, narrow face. His forehead was twice as wide as his jaw, and this made him look like a scholar. He was nine years older than I.

"It's my middle name, but it's an excellent name for a schoolteacher. Do you know the *Odyssey*?"

"I know pieces of it from the readers in school."

"I didn't think you'd been able to go to school," replied Mentor.

"Some in Kentucky and some in Indiana," I replied. Then I added, "The *Odyssey*? Sure, I remember it. Old Riney talked about it. Someone had been away from his home for twenty years because he'd been in a war and then couldn't get back."

"That's it."

"Tell me more about it."

Mentor started, "It begins with Telemachus, who is Odysseus's son, and who hasn't seen his father since he was two, when his father left for the Trojan War. Odysseus's home has been taken over by arrogant men who want to marry his wife. Everyone thinks he's dead since he's been gone for so long. Telemachus has no idea what to do. He's feeling powerless and alone. The goddess Athena appears to him in the form of an old man called Mentor."

Mentor stopped to see if I was still interested.

"So this Mentor becomes Telemachus's teacher?" I asked.

"Yes, but not like a teacher in school."

"How is he different?"

"It's not like teaching arithmetic or grammar. Mentor tells him stories. The most important part is that Mentor gives him the confidence to grow on his own."

"Is that what happens?"

"Yes. After all, he is the son of Odysseus."

I leaned on the table and edged closer to Mentor. "How does he get along with his father?" I asked.

"That's an important part of the story."

"So how do they get along?"

"In the beginning, Telemachus is very hesitant and weak. He knows his father would not be proud of him. He needs to grow up. His relationship with Mentor changes him. When his father appears at the end, he is ready to help Odysseus take on the suitors. He and his father stand side by side and kill them all."

We paused in our conversation.

I looked into the dying embers of the fire and said sadly, "I have so much to learn. Can you teach me?"

"What is it you want to learn?"

"I want to use words. I had a notion of studying grammar."

Mentor looked at me carefully and said, "I think that is the best thing you can do, and you should also be reading the Bible and the plays of Shakespeare."

"If I had a grammar book, I would begin now," I replied.

"There is none in this village. Vance, who lives about six miles from here, learned grammar from me two years ago. He has one. It's a Kirkham's. Vance will probably let you have it."

"I will go see Vance tomorrow."

"And you can come to the evening class starting next week. Annie Rutledge will join us."

The next day in the late afternoon, I decided to walk the six miles to Vance's place. I took the morning and afternoon time at Offutt's store, and Bill Greene offered to work the later hours. Vance and Mentor were friends, and Mentor gave me a letter to Vance introducing me.

It would take two hours to reach Vance's house and two hours to return to New Salem. I'd be going through open fields, then through the deep woods, and finally back into fields again. It was north toward the town of Petersburg. I'd take the old Indian trail through the woods. If I stayed for supper with Vance's family, I'd be returning in the dark.

I had no fear of being in the open fields or deep woods in pitch dark. That's all I'd known in Kentucky and Indiana. All my life I'd heard stories about bears and panthers.

There was one about a boy and a girl who had been told to pick berries in the woods. Their father was off hunting, and the mother was doing the washing in the creek. It was a day with sunshine and a breeze. It was the time just after the berries had ripened, so they were juicy and tasted especially sweet. The time passed quickly, and they ate some of the berries.

They heard a light rustling in the bushes behind them. Because they thought it was the wind, they paid no attention to it. They didn't hear it again, so they resumed the picking and tasting of the berries.

All of a sudden, out of the brush, a panther leaped toward them. It was larger than either the boy or the girl. The terrified little girl tried to run away, but she tripped on a tree root and fell flat on the ground. In a moment the panther was on her. He tore her little body to pieces.

Fortunately, earlier that morning, the little boy had fastened his tomahawk to his belt. He pulled it out and smashed it into the animal's skull. His blow was so forceful that he could not get it free. Then he fainted.

He awoke in pain because the beast tore large pieces of flesh from his legs before it died. Nearby were the remains of his dead sister.

Somehow I didn't believe all of that story. It was probably told to warn children about going too deep into the woods.

I set out from New Salem by crossing the Sangamon River in Jack Kelso's canoe. The current carried me west, and then, as the river turned to the north, I paddled to the shore. I hid the canoe in the thick brush, and started to walk across the open fields.

It was an Indian summer afternoon. The wind blew lightly over the prairie grass. Lowering on the horizon, the sun sent shimmers of waning light. A last burst of yellow-brown blossoms rose from the dying goldenrod. The leaves on the far trees, which had been green and yellow several weeks earlier, had now turned brown and begun to drop to the ground.

As I approached the trees, I spotted the old Indian trail and plunged into the forest. I was seized by a sudden spell of melancholy. I had experienced these feelings many times already in my life. Sometimes I would remember the careworn face of my mother, but I would also remember her kindly, soothing voice as she told Sarah and me the stories from the Bible. Sometimes I would see Sarah's face and remember how she took care of me when Papa left for Kentucky. Sometimes I thought of my brother Thomas, who lived only four days.

It was impossible to break free from these feelings. I just had to endure them, and they would depart as mysteriously as they had arrived.

Although the trail was narrow, I made good progress. My legs were long and powerful. I took large strides. The trail was not direct, but I trusted it. The Indians had carefully mapped these forest paths. Eventually I reached the northern edge of the forest and broke out into an open field that welcomed me with inviting twilight. The melancholy lifted as I looked up and saw the evening star.

Mentor's directions were simple, and I easily found my way to Vance's house. Vance was a large, cheerful fellow who welcomed me heartily. He introduced me to his wife and children and invited me to join them for supper. It was a meal of rabbit stew with potatoes and carrots pulled from the garden that afternoon. I told them the news about my friends in New Salem.

After the meal, Vance eased back into his chair and read Mentor's letter.

"So, has our friend Mentor roped you into one of his grammar classes?"

"Ain't so," I replied.

Vance eyed Mentor's letter again. Then he looked up at me.

"Says here the prettiest gal in town is coming. Is that the draw?"

"Nope," I said hesitantly.

Vance found his copy of Kirkham's and gave it to me. I said I'd return it as soon as I was finished, but Vance said there was no need and that I could keep it. He was sure I would put it to good use.

As the evening ended, I said I'd never forget Vance's generosity and kindness. He simply asked me to return the favor to someone else, and I set out into the night.

It was quite late, but with my copy of Kirkham's under my arm, I walked across the fields toward the woods. After a steady pace on the trail through the forest, I reached the open field just north of New Salem. The air was pure and I inhaled steadily. I could see my breath as I exhaled. Some of the houses of New Salem were recognizable on the distant hill.

I looked up and tried to find the constellations that I knew. I was familiar with the Great Bear and the Lesser Bear that some called the Dippers. Mentor had taught me to recognize Cassiopeia, which looked like the letter W. There was also a giant square with bright stars at each of the corners.

I loved the stars and wished I knew more about them. They would always be a great mystery. Were they a crafted pattern or were they simply random points of light?

I couldn't make up my mind. On such a night, I felt close to the world, but there were other times when I felt distant and alone.

I came to the riverbank and found the spot where I had hidden Kelso's canoe in the brush. I could see the current of the river in the moonlight. Leaves and small branches swept past the shore.

Just as I pulled back the shrubbery shielding the canoe, I heard a deafening harsh cry and a battering of the brush and air by the enormous wings of a great bird. It rose into the night, circled over the river, and croaked a threatening "rok, rok" at me. Then it hammered into the water near the bank with a thunderous splash.

I was not frightened, but I had been severely startled. I maneuvered the canoe out of the brush and onto the river as quickly as I could.

"I'm sorry," I called out to the bird. "I must have disturbed your nest."

Whether the bird responded to my voice or sensed the threat was passing, it replied to me with a softer "rok, rok."

The following evening I walked to the Grahams' house to have supper with Mentor and Sarah. Ann Rutledge was expected to come as well, but she was not invited to the meal. Mentor was instructing Ann in grammar, and he said she welcomed the suggestion that I join them.

Sarah was Mentor's childhood sweetheart. When she was ten and he was fifteen, he told her he loved her, and she rushed off and hid under her bed. It took Mentor several years to win her, but now they were happy companions.

As Sarah finished cooking, Mentor and I sat together at the kitchen table.

"So you walked to Vance's and back yesterday, and he gave you his Kirkham's?" inquired Mentor.

"Yes, he did," I replied.

"You walked back last night?"

"Yes. I have to ask you about one of the constellations."

"You are more interested in the stars than in grammar," teased Mentor as he looked up at me.

"I told you there are many things I want to learn."

"Which constellation do you want to know about?"

"It was toward the north, maybe more to the northeast I guess, and halfway down on the horizon. It was a large square of bright stars, not the brightest ones, but very bright."

I leaned my elbow on the table and ran my hand through my coarse, black hair. I focused intently on Mentor's explanation.

"That's an easy one," he responded. "It's the front half of Pegasus, the winged horse from Greek mythology. Underneath him are the stars that form his neck and head. He flies upside down."

"Upside down?"

"Yes, I suppose the ancients were not bound by reason when they looked up at the stars."

There was a knock on the door.

Sarah opened it and in walked a pretty young woman with a lovely smile. She was short, but under her cotton dress and woolen wrap was a full, attractive figure. She removed her cap, and out tumbled flowing blond hair. She had a round face with sparkling blue eyes.

"Why, Annie, we are delighted you will join us this evening," said Sarah, welcoming her to their home.

"Mr. Lincoln, you are acquainted with Miss Rutledge?" offered Mentor.

"Yes, I am," I said, trying not to appear awkward, but I was not sure I succeeded.

I had no reason to feel uneasy around her. She had been courted by several men in New Salem and become engaged to John McNeil, a prosperous businessman. While the women of the village thought she had made a good match, her father was not pleased because McNeil was twelve years older than Ann.

Ann looked directly at me. "My sisters and I have had the pleasure of Mr. Lincoln's company at our father's tavern. He is always welcome to stay with us."

Sarah led us over to the kitchen table. Ann followed like a young fawn, but I must have resembled a timid giraffe. We both seated ourselves and waited for Mentor, who had excused himself to use the backhouse.

He returned and asked us if we had brought our Kirkham's for the evening's lesson. Ann reached into her bag and confidently put hers on the table. I slumped in my chair with mine in my lap.

"Alright," said Mentor, "tonight we'll work on nouns—the difference between common and proper nouns. It's on page thirty-two. Abe, will you please read for us?"

I bent my head down toward my lap.

Mentor said, "Abe, you look like a large bird about to spear a fish. You can read it better if you put your book on the table."

I did what he wanted and started to read tentatively.

"The distinction between a common and a proper noun is very obvious. For example: *boy* is a common noun because it is a name applied to all boys; but *Charles* is a proper noun because it is the name of an individual boy. Although many boys have the same name, yet you know it is not a common noun, for the name Charles is not given to all boys."

"How logical," I noted and continued to read from the text.

It turned out it was logical. Grammar was a system that helped me to use language properly. I was embarrassed by all the mistakes I'd been making before I knew better.

———

James Rutledge had established a Literary and Debating Society in New Salem. The members were Rutledge and his son Robert, Mentor Graham, Jack Kelso, the town's two doctors—John Allen and Jason Duncan—Henry Onstot, and John McNeil. At the monthly meetings, a member gave a presentation on an important local or national issue. Then there was intense debate. The last two topics had been what to do about alcohol abuse and whether women should be allowed to vote.

On the evening of February 26, 1832, James Rutledge called the meeting of the society to order. It was held in the public room of the Rutledge tavern. This room included a large kitchen fireplace and a dining area that could also be used as a meeting space.

A fire crackled cheerfully in the fireplace, and several candles on the dining room table lit up the weathered faces of the members. They had trudged through a foot of snow to reach the Rutledge tavern. Once inside, they had huddled together around the fireplace.

This night was to be my initiation into the society. No one knew quite what to expect. Since I was known for my amusing stories like the one about Bill the drunk, they wondered if it could be light entertainment. It was possible the chairman might have allowed this to help me gain confidence in making a public address.

I had little experience speaking in public, but through reading the newspapers, I was well versed in public issues. Once, while working on William Butler's farm in Springfield, I had gone to a speech given by Peter Cartwright. Cartwright supported Andrew Jackson. After he spoke, I got into it with him since I'd become a Henry Clay man. Mr. Butler was impressed by how much I knew about Illinois politics, and he said I'd won the argument.

That same summer, Cousin John Hanks and I went to a meeting for two Democrats, Ewing and Posey, running for the state legislature. Cousin John thought Posey gave a poor speech, set up a box for me, and yelled out that I would give a reply. I talked about how to make the Sangamon River passable for steamboats. When I finished, Ewing asked me how I knew so much, and I told him it came from reading the *Sangamo Journal*.

"Welcome to the February meeting of the New Salem Literary and Debating Society," began Mr. Rutledge. He was a large man who was used to being in charge. He was gracious about it.

"You know the rules, but I will review them for Mr. Lincoln.

"Respectful behavior at all times, no references to the Almighty in argument, and the fine for inattention is three cents."

"Specific, please. Our guest should have an example," boomed out the voice of Jack Kelso. "When was the rule for inattention last applied?"

A heated discussion took place with no conclusion.

Finally, Onstot volunteered. "It was Mentor. Mentor fell asleep during McNeil's speech on the tariff. We had a hard time deciding if it was disrespect or inattention."

"Aye, boys, it was Mentor," agreed James Rutledge.

"And to what use was his fine put?" demanded Kelso.

"For the candles that provide us more light than some of our members' speeches," roared Rutledge.

When the laughter died down, Rutledge began the introduction of the evening's speaker.

"Tonight we welcome a young man who has been among us for only seven months. In that short time, he has become our friend. He has asked to join our society, and if his presentation tonight meets with your approval, we will extend him an invitation."

"And if it doesn't?" jeered Jack Kelso.

"Jack, always the joker," scoffed Onstot.

"If it doesn't, we'll send him over to Clary's Grove to get some training," said Mentor.

Rutledge ignored the interruption and continued, "Let us hear from Mr. Abraham Lincoln on internal improvements."

I rose to their hearty applause.

I was nervous, so I probably looked uncomfortable.

"It ain't the gallows, Abe," yelled Kelso.

"Shush, Jack," said Rutledge.

I was dressed in a dark green linsey-woolsey shirt and my standard blue pantaloons. Kelso told me later that I looked like a scarecrow from one of the New Salem gardens.

As I started, my voice was at a slightly higher pitch than usual, and I had forced my hands deep into my pockets. I could barely look at their expectant faces. Kelso had to suppress a grin. The general belief was that I would tell one of my yarns.

I gathered the courage to begin.

"Fellow citizens . . .

"As we meet tonight, I wish to talk to you about local affairs. There are changes coming that will transform our lives. From New York to Indiana, state legislatures are authorizing the improvement of roads, the clearing of rivers, and the construction of railroads and canals. These improvements in transportation will create economic opportunities which no person will deny. We will be able to export the surplus products of our farms and import what we need from elsewhere.

"How shall we proceed in Illinois?

"Without the fervent support of our state legislators, we shall lose this opportunity."

The members of the audience seemed stunned. I think they had seen me as an intelligent, but uneducated, yokel—a poor, awkward, transient lad with some ambition but little means of achieving it.

My hands came out of my pockets and sawed through the air as I illustrated my points.

"We must dedicate our resources to the improvement of the Sangamon River.

"To make the Sangamon navigable, we will need to cut through the necks of the peninsulas the river has created in its zigzag course, to remove the drifted timber, to remove the turf, and to dam up old channels upon the lower thirty-five miles of the river.

"What the cost of this work would be I am unable to say, but I believe the improvement of the Sangamon River to be vastly important and highly desirable to the people of this county.

"Our state legislature will have to provide for the financing of our internal improvements."

I added more details and background to my proposal for making the river more navigable, and I discussed my experiences of the past year that gave me the perspective from which to make this argument.

When I concluded, there was lively applause from the audience. As they continued to clap, Kelso was the first to stand. The others followed immediately. I was thankful. I had prepared carefully and I had rehearsed with Mentor, but I had not expected a response like this.

"Bravo, Abe!" cried out Onstot. One by one they came forward to offer their congratulations. They voted unanimously to make me a member of the society.

After the meeting ended, Mr. Rutledge invited me to stay at the tavern for the night, and I accepted.

The members bid us farewell and set off into the snow and the night. As so often happens after a snowstorm, the sky was clear. The moon shone brilliantly onto the white drifts.

Mr. Rutledge and I returned and sat in comfortable wooden chairs, which we drew up to the fireplace. We both stared into the waning flames without talking.

He spoke first.

"Abe, that was a fine speech you gave to the society this evening."

"Thank you," I replied.

"It showed that you had worked on it and practiced your delivery. It's what we've learned to expect from you."

The last light from the fire rippled across his kindly face.

"Thank you for making me a member," I said. "I wanted to prove myself to you and the others."

"We've noticed that about you. Either you've come a long way from when you first got here, or it was there all along. I tend to think it's the latter. Under that awkward bumpkin is a shrewd young man."

I didn't know what to say.

"Abe, we know you've studied up on this internal improvements issue," he continued.

"We need someone from New Salem to speak up for us and to represent us. There are local and state issues that are going to affect the future of this town. Dr. Allen, Sam Hill, and John McNeil have approached me about something. I'm with them completely. We'd like you to consider running for the state legislature."

I was so surprised I couldn't speak. My face must have shown my astonishment.

"Abe, don't take it like that. We wouldn't ask you if we didn't think you could do it."

"Mr. Rutledge," I said, "I'm honored that you and the others would think of me for something like that. I'm deeply honored, but I couldn't do it. I'd never get elected.

Nobody knows who I am. Beside that, you know I'm a Whig, and that's the wrong party around here."

"For the legislature, Abe," he returned, "everybody votes for the man and not the party. That won't stop them from voting for you."

"But, Mr. Rutledge, they don't know me."

"We disagree, Abe, and we all think that even if you don't win, you'd start to get known around here. It's the first step and we want you to take it. Annie tells me you've been taking long walks lately. Think it over on one of them."

I was still dazed. I'd been interested in politics ever since I started to read the newspapers in Indiana, but I never thought there was any way into it for someone like me.

"Alright, Mr. Rutledge, I'll think it over."

Although I was roused by Mr. Rutledge's invitation to run for the legislature, I also felt like Telemachus, Odysseus's son, in the story Mentor told me. I was hesitant and weak. I didn't know what to do.

When these thoughts stirred, I recalled the heart of the story. It was through his relationship with Mentor that Telemachus changed. Lawyer Brackenridge and Colonel Jones had been my mentors in Indiana. Mr. Rutledge, Bowling Green, Jack Kelso, and Mentor himself were becoming mentors for me here in New Salem. I could learn from them.

With their help, I could develop the confidence to grow on my own.

Chapter Eight

None of It Seems Right to Me

As dusky mountains please the eye
When twilight chases day;
As bugle-tones that, passing by,
In distance die away;

Annie was right. I was taking long walks around New Salem. When the feelings of melancholy drifted over me, I would head out over the open fields bordering the village and on into the surrounding forests. One of the paths led through the woods and onto an endless sweep of prairie grass. I sometimes walked all the way to Petersburg and back. On these walks I would sort through my thoughts.

For several days I tried to decide about running for the legislature. Many of the men elected were lawyers. That was because the legislature was where the laws were made. From the time I read the *Revised Statutes of Indiana* and then saw Mr. Brackenridge in court, I had been interested in learning the law. I was just so poorly educated that it seemed beyond me.

I talked it over with Bowling Green, the man I'd voted for as justice of the peace. He invited me to come to his courtroom. He told me that I could get started by writing simple documents like deeds and wills, but I was still spending all my time working in the store and doing simple jobs like clearing land, cutting brush, and splitting rails.

It got around the village that I might run for the legislature. The Clary's Grove boys thought it was a great idea because they could make fun of me, particularly when I was giving speeches. The boys were always up for a laugh. I didn't want to be the object of one of their pranks.

Finally, I decided to run. I knew I wouldn't win, but Mr. Rutledge was right. It was about getting started. I had argued with friends about issues in the newspapers. Back in Indiana, I had practiced giving speeches. I was starting to see myself as a public man.

Mentor and John McNeil helped me write a campaign announcement. It came out to five pages. The last part was the hardest to write.

> Every man is said to have his peculiar ambition. Whether it be true or not, I can say for one that I have no other so great as that of being respected by my fellow man, by making myself worthy of their respect. How far I shall succeed in achieving this ambition is yet to be developed. I am young and unknown to many of you. I was born and have ever remained in the most humble walks of life. I have no wealthy or popular relations to recommend me. My case is thrown exclusively upon the independent voters of this county, and if elected they will have given me a favor, for which I shall be unwavering in my labors to deserve. But if the good people in their wisdom shall see fit to keep me in the background, I have been too familiar with disappointment to be troubled by it.

Mentor and John changed some of the words and fancied it up a bit, but we kept most of what I had written.

On an April morning, now a year after I had seen New Salem for the first time, I was eating an apple for breakfast and talking with Rowan Herndon in the Rutledge tavern. If I had written that I would not be troubled by disappointment, I needed to heed my own words.

Denton Offutt's business ventures in New Salem failed. He closed the store, broke his contract with Rutledge and Cameron to operate the mill, left numerous debts, and skipped town. Even though my expenses were minimal, I was no longer employed, and I had nowhere to live. I could continue to do the odd jobs I hated, but that was not the step forward I wanted to take in my new setting.

As I was telling Row about this, we heard a commotion outside the door. A young man we did not recognize had ridden wildly into town. He called out for all the young men of New Salem to assemble and hear his news. When Row and I caught up with him on the main road, a large crowd circled the rider expectantly.

The young man stepped down from his horse and paused to collect himself.

"Governor Reynolds has sent me," he began. "He needs volunteers for the state militia. Black Hawk and a thousand Indians have crossed the Mississippi River. They are threatening our settlers and their families. We've got to protect our people and get rid of these savages for good. General Atkinson has three hundred soldiers, but he's told the governor he needs five times that many to fight Black Hawk. We need you to join. There'll be a muster in Richland the day after tomorrow."

I learned that the Sac and Fox Indian tribes once lived in what was now northwest Illinois. They lived peacefully until the pioneers and settlers started pushing into their lands. After signing a treaty that gave them the use of the land for the time being, they regretted it and fought with the British against us in the War of 1812.

When they lost the war, they left for Iowa. Now they were crossing back into Illinois to reclaim their land.

The volunteers for the state militia gathered at noon on April 21 in Richland. It was a gray, raw, early spring day. Richland was thirty miles west of New Salem and about the same size.

I went to Richland and volunteered because I wanted to find out about military life, because I needed the pay, and because I had nothing else better to do.

Jack Armstrong and many of the Clary's Grove boys had come too. Sixty-seven of us from New Salem would be mustered for the fight with Black Hawk and the Indians.

Shortly after noon, a large man with a reddish face and a bushy, black beard started yelling at us. He was wearing a frayed, dirty militia uniform. He stood with his legs slightly apart and eyed us skeptically. His voice droned on without expression.

"Your term of service is thirty days. You will be paid thirty-five dollars on May 20, 1832. You will have no leave. You are to furnish your own clothing and muskets. Your company will be supplied with ammunition. You are to provide us with the name of next of kin in the event of injury or death. You will be trained for three days before you march to join General Whiteside's brigade. You will abide by the code of conduct as enforced by your company commander. After you have taken the oath, you will meet by company to select a captain. The captain will appoint the first sergeant.

"I will now administer the oath."

He surveyed us as we stood before him. Our clothes were ragged, our faces scarred, and our muskets were rusty fowling pieces. The officer looked like he didn't envy the person who would have to lead this motley group.

"I will now give you the oath and you will repeat it.

"I do solemnly swear that I will bear true allegiance to the state of Illinois."

We mumbled his words back in unison.

"I will support the constitution thereof."

We repeated this.

"I will serve the state of Illinois faithfully in its military service for the term of thirty days unless sooner discharged."

Finally, he said, "I will observe and obey the orders of the officers appointed over me, so help me God."

He looked at the Clary's Grove boys as he said this.

We repeated this, and he congratulated us as new members of the Illinois state militia.

He gave us our next order.

"You will meet by company and elect your captains."

We were ordered to assemble by one of the large oak trees on the village green. The election was conducted by a young soldier who was serving under the officer who conducted the muster. He had an appealing manner, and we listened to him attentively.

"For the office of captain of your company, I will ask anyone who wants to submit his name for consideration to step forward."

The owner of a local saw mill stepped forward confidently.

The young man asked his name.

"William Kirkpatrick," he replied loudly.

"Do you wish to stand for election as captain of your company?"

"I do," said Kirkpatrick.

"Is there anyone else who wants to submit his name?"

There was a brief silence, but it was broken by Bill Greene, who said to Royal Clary, "We can't have that son of a bitch Kirkpatrick."

Without consulting anyone, Royal Clary yelled out to the crowd, "Abe Lincoln. We want Abe Lincoln to be our captain."

A loud roar of approval led by the Clary's Grove boys rolled over the assembly. Several of the men called out, "Stand forward, Abe."

I was standing next to John Rutledge. When my name was first proposed, I said softly, "No, I'm not right for it."

The Clary's Grove boys would have none of it. "Abe, Abe Lincoln!" they continued to whoop.

Finally, Royal Clary stepped over to me and Rutledge and gave me a friendly, but firm, shove toward the front. Others joined in and soon I was standing next to William Kirkpatrick.

"What is your name?" asked the young soldier.

"Abraham Lincoln," I replied.

"Do you wish to stand for election as captain of your company?"

I paused momentarily and then looked out over the men.

"Yes," I replied, "I do."

"Alright, then. We have two volunteers: Mr. Kirkpatrick and Mr. Lincoln. Here's how we will conduct the election."

He looked over at Kirkpatrick and me and asked us to stand farther apart.

"Those of you favoring the election of Mr. Kirkpatrick will now stand in line behind him. Those of you favoring the election of Mr. Lincoln will now stand in line behind him. No jabbering about this. No electioneering. Just get in line behind the man you want for captain."

Without much fuss, the men separated and formed into the columns behind Kirkpatrick and me. The number of men in my column was three times that of Kirkpatrick's.

At first, I couldn't believe it. I said to Bill Greene, "I'll be damned, Bill, but I've licked him."

Kirkpatrick scowled. He had been certain he would be chosen.

I turned to both columns. I felt my voice carrying strongly in the cool spring air.

"I'm honored. I'll do my best not to let you down."

"Captain Lincoln," the young soldier addressed me, "your first responsibility as captain of your company is to choose your first sergeant. You may deliberate and give me a name in the morning, or you may choose him now. Which do you prefer?"

"I will name him now," I replied. "I choose Jack Armstrong to be the first sergeant of our company."

Jack and I conducted training exercises for the Fourth Illinois Regiment of Mounted Volunteers. These took place near the town of Richland. The other ten companies from Sangamon County were training in the vicinity as well.

The cool, unpleasant weather gave way to several days of full sun and light spring breezes. We marched our company in columns all day long, shared meals by campfires, and slept out in the open fields. The spring stars shone brightly overhead.

In the evenings, along with the other company captains, the young soldier who conducted the election gave us instructions on military maneuvers. Jack and I used these to drill our company the following day.

The Clary's Grove boys did not take to military discipline.

I ordered, "Fall in."

One of them replied, "Go to the devil, sir."

I did not take offense. I knew the boys had no intention of bucking me. Strict military discipline could never be imposed on them. I believed that gradually they would come to accept it. I knew that if we were ever in danger, they would follow my orders willingly.

On the day before we were to begin marching west and then north to Rock Island, where Black Hawk and his warriors were thought to be, I was giving the men their last training exercise. Over an open field, we were parading in a column twenty across. At the far end of the field was a small gate through which the men would have to pass in order to march into an adjoining field. The column needed to turn endwise and pass through it three abreast.

As the men strutted closer and closer to the narrow gate, I panicked. Even though Jack and I had gone over it the night before, I forgot the specific instruction for this maneuver.

I had no idea what to do, but I remained calm.

"Halt!" I shouted. "This company will break ranks for two minutes and form again on the other side of the gate."

The men didn't seem to notice the hitch, but if they did, they were good enough to let it pass.

We moved out on our journey to Rock Island on the afternoon of April 25. For the next two weeks, our lives settled into the routine of breaking camp in the morning, marching by day, and setting up camp in the evening. Our route took us through impenetrable forests, unforgiving brush, swollen creeks and streams, and open prairie. Our overalls, which were already patched with foxing, grew more tattered each day. While all of us had known hardships, few of us were ready for the demands of this life. For many of the men, this was the first time they had been away from their homes.

At night we were exhausted. Camp life provided some relief. We were given beef, which we boiled, and we made crude forms of bread from the rations of flour. The boys foraged and brought back chickens that looked like skeletons and tasted like saddlebags. We played chess, checkers, and cards.

Camp entertainment was wrestling matches between the company champions. I represented the Fourth Illinois, winning all my matches but one. Lorenzo Dow Thompson defeated me in two falls, and the men lost their bets. They cried that Thompson had fouled me, but I told them, "Boys, the man threw me fair once, clearly so, and the second time, he threw me fairly, though not apparently so."

One night soldier Pot Greene told the men to get him a tomahawk and four buckets, and he would lead them to the officers' liquor supply. Without me knowing, they succeeded and stole enough wine and brandy to go around.

The next morning I ordered Jack to summon the men and form a parade. Some of the men were still drunk, and many of them could not be wakened. The other companies began the day's march, but we did not break camp until ten o'clock. After their first steps, I realized there was no choice but to let the drunken men sleep in the prairie grass. That night when the company finally marched into the evening camp, I accepted responsibility for our dereliction of duty and was placed under arrest. Fortunately, the punishment was not severe, and I was forced to carry a wooden sword for the next two days as a sign of our shameful conduct.

On May 13, we reached the Rock River. Illinois militia brigades under General Whiteside, including us, joined the United States Army soldiers under General

Atkinson. Atkinson ordered Whiteside's men to pursue Black Hawk. Although our company was not in the front, we were to follow up in the event of a battle.

All day long on May 14, we heard confusing reports of possible action. Governor Reynolds dispatched almost three hundred poorly trained recruits under Major Isaiah Stillman to confront Black Hawk and his war party. The Indians may have sent a small delegation to meet with the lead units of the militia. It may have been a trick to lull the militia into believing the Indians did not want to fight. Some men saw a white flag, but others didn't.

In the early evening, a small band of Black Hawk's warriors surprised Stillman and attacked his militia. There were casualties among the white men, but only three Indians were killed.

The next day, we were ready for possible action. The Indians were known for trickery. No one knew if Black Hawk would attack again. When we stopped for lunch, there was little conversation.

The order came to continue the march. Shortly afterward, we smelled the unmistakable odor of gunpowder. The order came to halt. Fifteen minutes later, a captain of the United States Army walked down the columns, identified himself, and asked to see me. We talked briefly. He then moved along the line to the next company.

I told our company, "Boys, we've been asked to cut over to that Indian trail by the trees. It will take us to the creek. There's no sign of Indians around. We've been given burial detail."

The boys, who had been tense all afternoon, now turned grim. We marched along the trail we were given. The smell of gunpowder now mingled with a putrid stench. The trail turned past the last clump of trees and led straight through the grass and brush to the side of the creek. We saw several figures standing at attention in the distance. Advancing toward them, we received salutes. No one spoke.

I led the boys forward. We came to the campground where Stillman's militia was slaughtered the night before. We came to bury the dead.

We now understood the reason for the stench. Twelve bodies, unrecognizable as individual soldiers, lay decomposing. They were mutilated. Several were beheaded. The detached heads were scalped. The white of the skull bone shone as a small circle in the black hair. The hair was matted with caked blood. The chest cavities of several bodies were open. Inside were mangled holes of broken ribs, ripped veins, and pools of drying blood. Their hearts had been removed. The ground was splashed with blood and bits of brains.

The work of the afternoon was to give these disfigured remains a proper burial. In between their labors, many of the boys, including their captain and first sergeant, vanished into the brush. To the sight of the massacre and the smell of the rotting corpses was added the sound of us retching as we paused from our grisly duty.

Later that evening in the glow of the waning campfire, Jack and I were sitting close to each other.

If someone had walked by, he would have seen a tall, thin man slumped over the diminishing flames, and another man, short and squat, with his head tilted reverently toward the ground.

"Abe, I seen the blood spurt and guts spring out from the hogs or chickens I slaughtered on the farm, and I ain't squirmy about it, but I ain't seen nothin' like I seen today. It's still with me."

"Reckon it'll stick with us all our lives, Jack," I replied.

"Why would them savages do something like that? If we'd've killed 'em, we wouldn't've tore 'em all up to hell like that. We ain't done it with the ones we killed."

I paused, stirred the fire slightly, and then said, "No, we respect their dead the same way we respect our own."

Jack grew livelier.

"I heard what them savages sometimes done, but I never expected what we seen today."

I peered away from Jack and into the fire. I was on the verge of sharing something that was painful to me.

"Jack, I never told you, but my grandfather was killed by a savage. My pa was right there. He saw it happen."

"Your grandpa?"

"It was Papa's dad, Abraham. That's where I get my name."

I looked up at the stars briefly. They seemed cold and distant.

"It was when my pa was young in Kentucky. A savage shot Grandpa when he and his boys were planting corn.

Uncle Mord was coolheaded. He and Uncle Josiah ran to the cabin. He sent Uncle Josiah for help. When an Indian in war paint came out of the woods to scalp Grandpa and steal Papa, Uncle Mord shot him through the heart. Papa used to tell that story more than any other."

"You got more reason than anyone else to hate the savages, but I don't hear you talking that way," Jack responded.

"None of it seems right to me, Jack."

———

Black Hawk and his warriors disappeared temporarily. Our company continued to give support to the companies who were pursuing the Indians. The boys were coming toward the end of their thirty days of enlistment, and they were grumbling about not having seen any action.

One morning while we were about to break camp, we were stunned and surprised by a strange visitor. An old Indian tottered out of the brush toward us, and the boys surrounded him angrily. I had to pry them away to find out the cause of this odd disturbance.

The Indian explained that he had a paper from General Cass that gave him free passage through the region.

While I examined the shabby paper, one of the boys called out, "We have come to fight the Indians, and, by God, we intend to do so. We should kill him."

Others echoed the idea and chanted, "Kill him. He's a rotten savage."

I stood between the men and our red-skinned visitor and said, "Boys, this must not be done. He must not be shot and killed by us."

Another of our soldiers shouted, "How do you know, Lincoln? The Indian is probably a damned spy. We should kill him. Kill him for what they done to our men."

I continued to resist their growing resentment and lust for blood.

Then came a charge from one of the boys, "Lincoln, this is cowardly on your part."

I did not grow heated easily, but this was it.

"If any man thinks I am a coward, let him test it."

I was aglow with rage, and I towered over them more than ever.

At this, the men backed off. I returned the paper from General Cass to the old Indian and escorted him away to the edge of the clearing.

"You may pass through this territory," I said to him. "Your paper says you are a member of a tribe that declares Black Hawk an enemy. Be careful as you travel. Black Hawk's warriors are near, and our own men are not always friendly."

I do not know if he understood me, but he thanked me and disappeared into the brush.

CHAPTER NINE

WHAT TO DO NEXT

And, freed from all that's earthly vile,
Seem hallowed, pure, and bright,
Like scenes in some enchanted isle
All bathed in liquid light.

The heat that descended from the naked, brutal sun of early August 1832 now shimmered upward from the parched ground. There was no breeze, but it appeared that the light and the air were in motion. The open ground of the prairie was baking. It had not rained for three weeks, and the long grass was turning brown.

The sweltering heat did not stop the citizens of Pappsville from flocking to the sale at the Knapp and Pogue store. Knapp and Pogue was one of several log houses that formed the small prairie town, eleven miles from New Salem. In addition to the mid-afternoon sale, another event was scheduled for slightly later in the afternoon. The twelve candidates running for the state legislature in Sangamon County had been invited to speak in a last appeal to the voters; the election canvass was to be held on August 6, three days later.

A makeshift platform for the speakers, several rickety boards resting atop bales of hay, had been erected in the open field behind the Knapp and Pogue store. Shortly before the event, the inhabitants of Pappsville received the disappointing news that, although several candidates had accepted the invitation to speak, only I would appear that afternoon.

David Smith, the leading citizen of Pappsville, stood on the speaker's platform and asked for order. Given the circumstances, it was surprising that the crowd numbered close to fifty people. As Smith tried to get their attention, he realized that the audience was rowdier than usual. Perhaps it was the free drinks of whiskey that Knapp and Pogue had provided to drum up trade for the sale. Perhaps it was my rowdy friends who would not quiet down for the opening remarks.

I accompanied Smith to the platform, and I'm sure I seemed out of place and awkward in the afternoon sun. I was sweating profusely into my frayed blue-and-white striped cotton shirt. My blue denim pants left several inches of my calves exposed above my shoes. My face was deeply red, not the burnt brown of the men and women who worked in the fields at this time of year. I held my straw hat in my hands as Mr. Smith introduced me to the crowd.

"Ladies and gentlemen," called Smith, and the raucous conversations died down only slightly. He continued, "For today's candidate's forum, I am delighted to present our candidate for the state legislature, Mr. Abraham Lincoln from New Salem."

At my introduction, the Clary's Grove boys, who came with me on each of my campaign appearances, cheered loudly. They continued well past the polite length for this kind of demonstration, and no gesture or holler from the moderator could quiet them. As I began to speak, they gradually subsided.

I could feel myself hurrying the words, "My friends, thank you for that warm introduction and for giving me the opportunity to appear before you this afternoon." At this point I stopped to brush my unkempt hair out of my sweating face.

"Fellow citizens, I have been told that some of my opponents have said that it was a disgrace to the county

of Sangamon to have someone who looks as I do stuck
up for the legislature. Now I thought this was a free
country. That is the reason I address you today. Had I
known to the contrary, I should not have consented
to run.

"Gentlemen, I have just returned from the Indian
war. My personal appearance is rather shabby and dark.
I am almost as red as those men I have been chasing
through the prairies and forests and rivers of Illinois."

At this point a huge fight broke out in the crowd.
Row Herndon took offense at something a person from
Pappsville said about my appearance and punched
him in the face. This set off an explosion. Several men
from Pappsville jumped on Row and began to pummel
him. I jumped off the speaker's platform, pushed aside
people in the crowd like bowling pins, and then jumped
into the fight. One by one I picked up the attackers
from Pappsville and threw them aside. I pitched one of
them out into the field. After rescuing Row and ending
the disturbance, I returned to the platform and, after
pausing to wipe my face with a handkerchief, continued
my speech.

"Fellow citizens, I presume you all know who I am—I
am humble Abraham Lincoln. I have been solicited by
many friends to become a candidate for the legislature.
My policies are short and sweet, like the old woman's
dance. I am in favor of a National Bank, I am in favor of
the internal improvement system, and a high protective
tariff. These are my sentiments and political principles.

If elected I shall be thankful; and if not, it will be all the same."

Four days later I learned that I finished eighth among the thirteen candidates for the legislature. While I was discouraged, my friends urged me to take heart when we learned that of three hundred votes cast in the New Salem district, I received 277.

My friends' good will couldn't sustain my spirits. The electoral loss brought back the melancholy. When it finally eased away, I was left with an overall uncertainty about what to do next. It was now early October.

I set out on a mid-morning walk. The sky was slate gray. With a sporadic breeze from the north, the air cut against me with a slight chill.

I headed east, which meant I had to use Jack Kelso's canoe to cross the river. At the riverbank, I pulled the old and battered canoe into the water. I noticed a solitary heron who was spearing minnows in the marshy shallows.

I paddled over the Sangamon, pulled the canoe onto the opposite shore, pushed it under a convenient willow bush, and set out over the fields toward the woods. This cheerless day was brightened slightly by the yellows and oranges of the turning leaves. As I neared the oak trees at the edge of the forest, I saw the feverishly active squirrels gathering acorns for the winter. I was not the only one who was observing this fall ritual. I happened to look at the sky again, and there was a majestic hawk circling closely above.

With that I plunged into the woods. This was the

path that led to the prairie grass beyond the forest. I strode along the trail and soon came to the clearing, which beckoned with the brown grasses of October. Here I slowed and my thoughts began to churn.

What could I find here that would allow me to stay? Could I continue to depend on the kindness of Jack and Hannah, of Mentor and Sarah, of the Rutledges, the Onstots, and the Kelsos?

Henry suggested that I apprentice as a blacksmith. It would be steady work, but would it be what I wanted? Could I accept Bowling Green's invitation to come to his courtroom and learn about the law? I hadn't read or learned enough.

These people welcomed me, and they became my friends and my teachers.

Mentor helped me to find a Kirkham's. He got me started, and then I learned grammar on my own. I said to Bill Green, "If that is what they call a science, I'll subdue another." I'd started reading the Scriptures and history, science, and religion. Jack gave me Burns and Shakespeare, but I still had so much to learn.

Could I be patient? If I'd been elected to the legislature, I would have earned a small stipend. It would have been a start. That was all I wanted.

Something I discovered was that store owners in small towns were often very successful. People from all around came to a store for the things they needed. They talked about their farms, the weather, and politics. If I could find a partner, my friends would take notes on credit, and I could get started as a storekeeper.

Sam Hill and John McNeil operated the most successful store in New Salem. James and Row Herndon tried unsuccessfully to compete with Sam and John. Reuben Radford established his own store and was just beginning to eke out a profit when disaster struck.

In the late fall, James and Row decided to sell, and William Berry—who served in our company during the Black Hawk War—and I purchased their store on credit. Shortly after this, the Clary's Grove boys destroyed Reuben's store because he had limited the amount of liquor he would sell to them. After that, Reuben was ready to quit and sold what was left of his store and his inventory to Bill Greene, who, in turn, sold it to Berry and me. Reuben's repaired store was preferable to the one we purchased from the Herndons, and in late 1832, the second Lincoln and Berry store was open for business.

I suppose there were warning signs from the beginning. I was better at telling stories and talking politics with our customers than I was at collecting their bills. During the lulls, I propped myself on the counter, took out a book, and read until the next customer appeared. In the fall of 1833, I let Berry, who was drinking up his share of the meager profits, apply for a license to sell liquor by the glass. That would turn us into a grocery like the store Bill Clary operated near the mill.

On a blustery January day, Bill pushed open the door to our store, ushered in both himself and a gust of howling wind, stomped the snow off his boots and onto the floor, and then rubbed his hands on his ruddy cheeks. He spied me on the counter, absorbed in my book.

"No, Bill, we have no return on your investment for you today," I said without looking up at my visitor.

"I expected as much," replied Bill, "but if Berry insists on selling liquor, I may have to get a share of those profits before this enterprise is ruined."

"Bill," I said while continuing to read, "this entire village is headed for ruin if they can't widen the river or run the railroad line near us or build a road from here to Springfield."

"Abraham, that's not the problem and you know it. What are you reading?"

"It's *The Age of Reason* by Thomas Paine."

"My God, isn't it enough to let the devil do his work with Berry's infernal drinking?" argued Bill. "Why are you reading that heresy?"

"You must hear some of it," I countered.

"No, Abraham, I'd rather have a yarn than that nonsense."

I put my book aside and sat forward on the counter.

I began, "How about the one about the old Baptist preacher?"

He nodded in approval.

"He was dressed in a shirt and pants of coarse linen. The pants had bag legs and but one button at the waist with no suspenders, and the shirt had sleeves and one button on the collar. He raised up in the pulpit and took his text thus: 'I am the Christ whom I shall represent today.'

146

"About this time a blue lizard ran up his legs. The old man began to slap away on his legs but missed the lizard and it kept getting higher up. He unbuttoned his pants at one snatch and kicked them off, but the thing kept on up his back. The next motion was for the collar button of his shirt, and off it went.

"In the church was an old lady. She took a good look at him and said, 'Well, if you represent Christ, I am done believing in the Bible.'"

Bill guffawed, but his religious sensibilities returned and he chided me. "I wouldn't tell that one around Sam Hill. He'd run you out of town."

I reached back and picked up my book. "And now I will read you some passages from Thomas Paine."

Bill winced.

With a smile, I continued to torment him. "Bill, you must listen to this."

A gray cat with dark gray stripes and gleaming green eyes jumped up on the counter and then onto my lap. I stroked it with one hand and read from the book with the other. I read slowly.

"I do not believe in the creed professed by the Jewish church, by the Roman church, by the Greek church, by the Turkish church, by the Protestant church nor by any church that I know of. My own mind is my own church.

"All national institutions of churches, whether Jewish, Christian, or Turkish, appear to me no other than human inventions set up to terrify and enslave mankind, and monopolize power and profit."

Bill looked up at me. "Are you finished?"

"For the moment," I replied.

"Surely, Abraham, you do not believe what you have read to me."

"Oh, but Bill, I surely do."

"No, you cannot."

"But I do."

"So you don't believe that the Scriptures are the Word of God?"

"I do not."

"And you don't believe in the Virgin birth?"

"I do not."

"Any you don't believe in the divinity of Christ?"

"I do not."

"Abraham, what is your religion?"

"Bill, my religion is 'Holy Willie's Prayer.'"

"Oh, no, what is that?"

"It's a poem by Burns."

"And where did you find this?"

"Jack Kelso showed it to me."

Carrying the cat under one arm, I leapt off the counter, waved my other arm in the air, and spoke in the Scots dialect with passion and fury.

"O Thou that in the Heavens does dwell,

Wha, as it pleases best Thysel,

Sends ane to Heaven an' ten to Hell

A' for Thy glory

And no onie guid or ill

They've done before Thee!"

"I do not believe in a God who would condemn anyone to eternal damnation."

"Stop!" cried Bill. "Lincoln, you are an infidel! You will never be elected if you keep talking this way."

"Alright, Bill, for you I will keep this to myself. But I need your help with something else that has nothing to do with elections."

"What's that?" he asked.

"You know last month we became a grocery."

"Yes."

"Well, it was a mistake."

"I warned you, Abraham."

"Not only is Berry rarely sober, but what he does collect from his drunken friends funds his own habit."

"The perils of selling liquor," said Bill sharply.

"That fellow Thomas is in here most nights drinking himself into a stupor. He lives down toward Clary's Grove and either Berry or I have to walk him home through the woods because he's afraid of ghosts."

"I haven't heard of any around here. Have you?"

"No, but that's not the point. It makes no difference to Thomas."

"Well, then, what can you do?"

"I've got an idea that might cure both Thomas and Berry."

Bill looked at me dubiously.

"I've got Berry in on a plan for tonight. I will walk Thomas home and halfway into the woods, Berry will jump out at him in a sheet and frighten the bejesus out of Thomas. What I need is for you to play ghost with a sheet and jump out at Berry about a minute later. That should do the trick."

"Alright, Abe, it'll be cold out there, but it's worth it if it'll cure Berry and this other fool."

We did play our joke on Thomas and Berry, and while it worked and caused Thomas to change his ways and leave New Salem for home before dark, it did not cure Berry of his love of drink.

We were inept at running the store. I was more involved in my reading and learning, and Berry was drinking himself to death. Finally, the store winked out. I was left with no employment and deep in debt. If my friends could not intercede on my behalf, I would have to leave New Salem.

———

In the village of New Salem, Sam Hill was the postmaster. It was not a duty that he liked even though the post office was located in his store. Sam was more interested in serving the men their liquor than in telling the ladies their letters had arrived. Not only was one profitable, but the other was a tiresome chore.

The person who sent the letter did not pay postage. The postmaster's job was to deliver a letter or a newspaper and then collect the fee for postage from the person who received it. He had to keep careful records of his receipts, and of course, Sam had to keep these documents separate from the inventory and sales records he kept for his store.

My friends persuaded Sam to give up his position. They then pressed for my appointment. Andy Jackson had been elected president in 1832, but because the job of postmaster was not important, my Whig politics were overlooked. I was appointed postmaster on May 7, 1833. Since the mail arrived twice a week in New Salem, it brought a small stipend, but it was a start. I was thrilled with one part of the job—I could read all the newspapers that came for the New Salem residents.

On a late spring afternoon, I was at my desk in Sam's store. I was sorting through the mail that had arrived earlier in the day when Ann Rutledge stood before me and asked anxiously whether a letter had come for her.

"No, Annie, there's no letter for you in this morning's post," I responded.

Her face, which was always so sweet and cheerful, faded into disappointment and sadness.

"Why, Annie, is anything the matter?"

"No, Abe, you are kind to ask, but there is nothing you can do."

She smiled at me but left abruptly. For the next month, this scene repeated itself twice a week, until one afternoon, she looked at me and burst into tears. I rose from the desk, moved toward her, and held her in my arms. Her crying continued and then quietly subsided. I felt her chest first heave with emotion and then gently settle back into more rhythmic breathing. She rested quietly in my arms. No one was in the store so neither of us was embarrassed. Gradually, Ann pulled away from me and regained her composure.

"Abe, you know I am engaged to John McNeil. You know that he left for the East. He planned to see his family and bring them to New Salem. We would then be married.

"What you do not know is that McNeil is not his proper name. It is McNamar. He changed it when he came west. His father failed in business. John left and didn't want his father to know where he had gone. He wanted to be successful and return with enough money for his family. He has done that and gone to them, but my entire family does not believe he will return. They do not trust a man who has changed his name. He wrote me faithfully at first, but now he has not written for over a month. You know I have come here hoping to hear from John. It is just so hard. I am beginning to doubt him myself."

"Annie, I have known John to be a man of his word. I do not believe he would forsake you," I said.

"Oh, Abe, thank you for those kind words, but maybe I shouldn't have trusted you with that secret."

"Annie, I've seen you walking in the late afternoon and early evening. Would you like some company?"

"Oh, Abe, there's nothing I'd like better."

Two days later we met at the Rutledge tavern in the late afternoon. It was mid-June and we were favored with the sun lowering in the west and a balmy breeze from the east. The summer heat and humidity, which could tiptoe into the days of late May and early June, had not yet made their appearance.

I asked Ann where she would like to walk, and she replied that her favorite spot was the open field on the eastern shore of the river.

As we meandered down the hillside to the Sangamon, we must have made an incongruous pair—I towered above her by over a foot. We looked like a stork and a plump little woodcock. She put me at ease by saying she liked looking up at me.

We climbed aboard Kelso's canoe, paddled it out into the river, hid the canoe in the brush on the other side, and set out to the east. As the sun sank into the horizon of the trees to the west, we walked slowly through the open field toward the forest. The field was covered with early summer wildflowers. From the bordering forest we could hear the early evening call of the whippoorwill.

Our conversation flowed easily. Perhaps this was because I knew Ann was betrothed. I felt as if I were a protective older brother.

"Abe," she asked, "what will you do next?"

"I will run again for the legislature—although it won't be until a year from August."

"Father says you'll win next time and that Mr. Stuart will help you."

"Yes, he's been asking me to come see him in Springfield. We were in the same company when I re-enlisted last summer. We've become friends. He thinks I should study law."

"What do you think?"

"I'm not ready for it yet, Annie. There's so much I don't know, but I'm working on it every day."

"What will you do until next August?"

"Calhoun needs an assistant surveyor. I've never done something like that, but I could learn. Mentor told me he'd teach me the figuring for it. The only problem is that

Calhoun is a Democrat, and they're not sure he'd take me on."

"They seemed to get over that when they made you postmaster."

"What about you, Annie?"

"I want to go to the female college in Jacksonville."

"Why, that would be just the thing for you!"

"Father thinks I might be able to do it if he makes enough money from selling the tavern."

"Why does he want to do that?"

"You know we are living on a farm up in Sandridge. He thinks the town is gradually going to die. Not right away, but sooner rather than later. He says the legislature, even with you in it, Abe, will never put up the money to straighten and widen the river. He wants to be closer to Petersburg. He thinks that's the coming place."

"Who will buy the tavern?"

"He says maybe the Trents or maybe Henry Onstot."

"I've felt at home here for the first time in my life, and now your father says the whole town is getting ready to die."

"It won't happen right away, and maybe he's wrong. We'll just have to see."

As we walked and conversed, the shadows of twilight began to fall around us. It was time to return. The light of the rising moon shone over the silhouette of the forest to the east. An owl called softly in the distance. We could hear the dogs from the town barking in the clear evening air.

"Abe, thank you for being with me today and tonight," she whispered as she pulled away from me and began to walk back toward the river and the town.

———

James Rutledge did sell the tavern in New Salem. Among several offers, he chose Henry Onstot's. Henry's offer was slightly lower than the Trents', but Mr. Rutledge believed Henry would maintain it as a tavern and guesthouse. The tavern was one of the places where I occasionally stayed.

In the early morning hours of November 13, 1833, I was sleeping soundly in the guest quarters. Earlier, during the day, I had walked to the town of Petersburg, and walked back to New Salem in the evening.

At three o'clock in the morning, Onstot burst into the guests' sleeping room and roused me with a fury. "Abraham," he screamed, "arise! The day of the judgment has come."

Holding a candle that showed his wild, almost crazed face, Onstot stared at me and cried, "Come outside and await your fate."

Alarmed, I threw on my pants, shirt, coat, and boots and accompanied him to the door and then out into the biting cold of a late fall night.

When I looked up at what I thought would be utter darkness, I could only marvel. From a central point west in the dome of the sky radiated not a shower, but a storm of streaks, brighter and wider at the head but narrower at the tail, before they burnt up into the darkness. I knew what they were. I had seen single meteors flash across the night sky, and I had eagerly awaited the meteors of mid-August each year, but I had never seen anything like this. There were thousands of blinding streaks racing across the sky. The town was illuminated well beyond the shadowy glow from a full moon. It was as if the sky were being shredded with the artillery fire from celestial armies.

Onstot was undone. He believed without doubt that this was the end of the world.

I was steadier.

"Look, Henry," I cried, "the familiar constellations are there behind it. It is a meteor storm coming from Leo, but there is Orion with the bright stars in his shoulder and knee. There is Sirius in the Great Dog, and there are the Dippers and the North Star. They are fixed and true in their places."

I put my arm on Henry's shoulder to comfort him.

"I do not know what it signifies," I said, "but I believe the world will be here tomorrow morning."

Henry was reassured to learn that there was an explanation for this terrifying event.

"Abe," he said, "now that I know what it is, I've never seen anything so beautiful."

CHAPTER TEN

ABRAHAM'S TRIAL

The friends I left that parting day,
How changed, as time has sped!
Young childhood grown, strong manhood gray,
And half of all are dead.

People in New Salem talked about the meteor storm for weeks. Although I was certain it had been a natural event, others looked to the Book of Revelation for an answer. I could not find an explanation in any of the science books that Jason Duncan and John Allen loaned me.

I continued with my reading and acquired a copy of Blackstone's *Commentaries on the Laws of England* at an auction. Since childhood I had read everything aloud, which meant that I moved through the text slowly, but I read Blackstone at only a snail's pace. I often reread a passage several times. Finally though, I felt comfortable with Bowling Green's offer to come to his court.

He held the sessions in the dining area connected to his kitchen. The room was large enough for a table, where he presided, and several chairs that accommodated the defendant, the lawyers, and the witnesses. He weighed nearly three hundred pounds and wore a linen shirt and denim breeches that were supported with one suspender. When he laughed heartily, which was often, his belly shook underneath his shirt. He called it his "pot" because it reminded everyone of a jelly pot.

He was called Esquire Green because that was how he referred to himself. When I got to know him better, he told me to call him "Squire." He'd come to New Salem from North Carolina by way of Tennessee, where he had met and married his wife, Nancy. His house was half a mile north of the village.

I decided I was ready to attend the court sessions. I sat in the back quietly observing. Most of the cases involved debts, boundary disputes, or theft.

The procedures were simple ones, but sometimes it was hard to know who was telling the truth.

There was one case where I was a witness.

The shoemaker, Peter Lukins, charged that Martin Waddell, the hatter, had never paid him in full for a pair of boots.

I was sitting in the background when Lukins talked to his attorney and told him to call me to the stand as a character witness.

I was sworn in and took one of the chairs for the witnesses.

Lukins's attorney began, "Mr. Lincoln, how long have you lived in New Salem?"

"It's been over a year, sir," I replied.

He continued, "Young man, my client tells me that you have a reputation for being forthright, that you are highly respected in the town, and that you were recently a candidate for the state legislature."

"And we hope he'll run and win next time," interjected Esquire Green.

I appreciated this because Bowling Green was a Jackson supporter and a leader of the Democratic Party in the county.

"How well do you know the plaintiff?" asked the attorney.

"Reasonably well," I replied.

"Please state what you know as to the character of Mr. Lukins."

This was a moment of difficulty for me, but I had no choice.

"Well, sir," I said, "he is called Lying Pete Lukins."

Esquire Green was convulsed with laughter. He rolled back and forth in his chair, pulled out a worn handkerchief, and held it to his eyes to wipe away the tears. He had to pull himself together to continue the proceeding.

This gave Lukins's attorney the chance to think quickly.

"Mr. Lincoln, would you believe Mr. Lukins under oath?"

I thought for a second, and then I said, "Ask Esquire Green. Mr. Lukins has testified before him many times."

Esquire Green thought for a moment and then said without hesitation, "I never believe anything he says unless someone swears the same thing."

Bowling Green thought I was ready to try a case. Of course, I had no experience and I had not studied the law in earnest, but he encouraged me and said the time had come.

"The Trent brothers have filed a writ of replevin against Jack Kelso for the return of a young pig that they say belongs to them," he told me. "Jack will represent himself, but the Trents don't want to and they can't afford a lawyer. Will you take the case for them?"

"Is that fair to them?" I asked.

"It's not complicated. You just have to talk to them, build your case, and then line up your witnesses. Your opening and closing statements will be brief. It will be over before you know it."

The day came and we all assembled in the esquire's courtroom. The Trents were angry that Jack hadn't just given it back, but Jack was jaunty as ever. I had brought two witnesses who sat together quietly. I wasn't nervous because I had prepared carefully and the evidence was clearly on our side. It was a little strange opposing Jack in the courtroom since we had become good friends. The esquire called us into session and asked me to begin.

"Your honor, this case is a simple one. As we all know, hogs wander through our town at will. Somehow, at the end of the day, they find their way home. On June 8 of this year, the three hogs owned by the Trent brothers returned, but they were missing a shoat that had been thrown earlier in the spring. Several days later, they found their shoat in Jack Kelso's pen. When they asked Jack to return it, he told them it belonged to him and to go to hell."

This caused the jovial esquire to start laughing and his pot to quiver.

"I will call two witnesses," I continued, "who will testify that the shoat in question belongs to the Trent brothers. The evidence is clear. The shoat must be returned to its rightful owners."

"Thank you, Mr. Lincoln. Mr. Kelso, your opening statement, please."

Jack rose with determination. He strode around the room like Don Quixote charging at the windmills. Mostly, he addressed his remarks to the esquire.

"Your honor, a few days after the date cited by the counsel for the plaintiff, I was leaning on the gate of my hog pen, and my neighbors, the Trent brothers, sitting right here to your left, marched up to me and yelled like drunken loons that my shoat, the little fellow that almost died but that I had nursed back to health, belonged to them. 'Utter nonsense,' I told them, and a few other things as well.

"Now the counsel for the plaintiff has informed us that our hogs roam freely throughout the village, and this is certainly true, but what he does not tell us is that many of our hogs and shoats look very much alike. It takes a polished eye, or an astute owner, one that has raised his hogs as if they were his children, and mind you, I have no children other than these animals, which I have nurtured from birth."

"What's the point, Jack?" bellowed the esquire.

"The point, your honor," said Jack, "is that the Trent brothers are mistaken, to put it kindly, and that if they could recognize the difference between shoats, they would apologize to me and the court for putting us through this nonsense. If we were to show the Trents two butterflies or two buttercups, do you think they could tell the difference between them?"

"Enough, Jack," retorted the esquire. "Mr. Lincoln, you will present your witnesses."

I had foreseen that Jack would try to win the case with bluster, and as I questioned the witnesses, I established that it was indeed possible to tell the difference between animals that looked very much alike. When twice Jack passed up the opportunity to cross-examine, I knew for sure there was nothing to his defense.

We both gave brief closing statements, and after making a few notes, the esquire said he would rule on the case momentarily.

What formality he observed came when he issued a ruling. He sat up in his chair and spoke deliberately.

"The two witnesses we have heard have sworn to a lie. I know this shoat, and I know it belongs to Jack Kelso. The writ of replevin is denied, and I decide this case in Kelso's favor."

I was stunned. When everyone left Bowling Green's house, I lingered behind.

"How could you, Squire?" I stammered.

"You'll get over it," he replied.

"But Jack Kelso is one of your best friends. You can't do something like that."

"You thought your evidence was clear and tight, Abe," he counseled, "but you have to realize not all witnesses are reliable. I know that shoat is Jack's. It wanders up here constantly. I've had to take it home to him a few times. If your witnesses were not lying, they were simply mistaken. Jack is right. It is very hard to tell them apart. The first duty of the court is to decide cases justly and in accordance with the truth. As for Jack being my friend, you'll learn that you put all that aside when the court is in session. If you can't, you have no business being a lawyer or a judge. You took a case opposing your good friend. He won't hold it against you. You are learning, Abe. Don't get ahead of yourself."

Esquire Green was right. After our encounter in the courtroom, Jack Kelso and I remained close friends.

Jack had a pot belly, a round face, twinkly blue eyes, and a scraggily white beard. He was bald but for a few strands of white hair that flew out from the sides and back of his head.

He had no profession and most of New Salem regarded him as incurably lazy, but he was a superb hunter and his smokehouse was never empty. He was equally skilled at fishing, and he always came back from an afternoon by the river with a large bass or catfish for dinner.

I did not like fishing, but I loved to sit with Jack on the banks of the Sangamon. In his loud, melodic voice, he recited verses from Burns and soliloquies from Shakespeare as he waited for bites, and I looked out at the river and let the words roll over me.

In the spring of 1834, Jack invited me to join him as he opened his fishing season. The weather that April afternoon was unseasonably warm. Clouds had rolled in after a morning of sunshine, and it felt as if a late afternoon thunderstorm was brewing.

Jack and I set out in the canoe for the far shore of the river. From my perch in the front, I looked back at him and asked, "Why do we always go to the far side?"

"Can't rightly say," he replied. "Maybe the channel or the water temperature suits 'em more, maybe the flies like it over there, maybe the shadows—maybe all of that or none of it or some of it."

We pulled the boat ashore and found a spot from which Jack could fish and where I could stretch my legs over the bank and sit and lie back on the cushion of wild grass.

At a leisurely pace, Jack took out a pouch with earth in it and poked around until he found a white brown insect grub that he used to bait his hook. His rod was an old fishing pole, but it had served him well over the years. The line had a small lead weight and a wooden bobber. He set the line several feet out into the river and sat back next to me on the riverbank.

"Well, my young friend," he began, "what ails you today?"

I responded cheerfully, "Nothing ails me, Jack. I'm biding my time."

"I know you too well, Abe. That's the last thing you are good at!"

"Well, you're right. I'm counting the days until I can declare for the state legislature and start the campaigning."

"And when is that?" he asked.

"I'll declare in June and the election is the first week in August."

"Most people think you'll win this time," asserted Jack.

"It's not a sure thing by any means. I'm better known,

but the Democrats have the votes."

"You won't win any votes with your infidel views. You can thank Sam Hill for putting that paper you wrote against Christianity into the fire."

"Jack, it's what I believe, or shall we say, it's what I don't believe."

"Did you tell Parthena Hill that when we die it is the last of us?"

"Isn't that what you think, Jack?"

"Abe, I don't think about it. We won't find out until we're gone. I'm content to wait."

At this point the bobber sank beneath the surface, and the pole was almost jerked out of his hands. He played with the line, gently tugging it from time to time. He let the fish fight itself out and then gradually pulled it to shore. It was an enormous bass. Jack held the fish firmly, carefully detached the hook from inside the white mouth, reattached the fish to a metal clip on a small round piece of wood, and then threw it back toward the river. Jack tied the device to a tree root that extended from the riverbank. He rebaited his hook and plopped the line and the bobber back into the slow-moving current.

"Abe, you'll have to come to dinner tonight to help us finish off this old fellow. He had to have been a survivor, but how strange that he took that hook just as we were deciding whether or not God exists. Do you see a sign in that?"

"Not really," I retorted. "That old fish was just ready

to be our dinner."

Looking up at the sky, I quoted, "Do you see yonder cloud that's almost in shape of a camel?"

Jack addressed the river in an aside, "Your noble son is mad."

He then added his line, "By the mass, and 'tis like a camel, indeed."

I continued, "Methinks it is like a weasel."

Jack followed, "It is backed like a weasel."

"Or like a whale?" I asked.

"Very like a whale," finished Kelso.

Then he added, "You know, Abe, I was sitting on this riverbank last summer and I was wondering whether I could memorize every line in Hamlet—I know half of it already—and then go through the rest of my life speaking only lines from Hamlet."

"Well, if you added Macbeth, you might be able to do it," I answered, and then my mood suddenly changed and I cried, "Oh, Jack, why are they all so noble, so misguided, and so miserable at the end?"

"Probably because they're exactly like us," said Jack.

"Are we noble, Jack?"

"Of course we are. . . . 'What a piece of work is a man! How noble in reason! How infinite in faculties! In form and moving how express and admirable! In action how like an angel! In apprehension how like a god! The beauty of the world, the paragon of animals.'"

"Hamlet and Macbeth—how admirable, how flawed, and how tragic," I responded.

"And how alone," said Jack.

"What?"

"Yes, Abe, how alone," repeated Jack.

I leaned forward and covered my face with my hands. A large gray-backed bird swooped down from the sky and landed in the river just to the side of us. It drifted over to the riverbank and then stood in the shallows by the clumps of emerging grass. As the bird spied Jack's large fish, it cawed a lusty "rok, rok."

"Easy, big fella," said Jack. "That one's not for you."

The bird gave him a curious look and then turned away, surveying the eddying water close to the shore.

I asked Jack, "That's a blue heron, isn't it?"

"It is. They're common around here, as you have no doubt noticed."

"Yes, but is it possible to tell them apart?"

"They probably do, but I'm not sure we can. Why do you ask?"

I looked carefully at the bird.

"I wonder if the bird I keep seeing could be the same one."

"So you think this bird has a relationship with you?"

"I wouldn't go that far."

"Well, Abe, if nothing else, you and this heron sure look alike. Your hair is mussed up most times just like its feathers. You both are long-legged creatures, and it stoops over just like you do."

"Mentor says it may be a sign."

"Of what?"

"He doesn't know. He says that in Book Ten of the

Iliad, Odysseus and Diomedes volunteer to spy behind the Trojan lines and ask for the protection of the goddess Athena."

I paused, took a deep breath, and then began to recite:

> "Just then, in sign she favored their intent,
> A long-wing'd heron great Athena sent."

"So Mentor thinks this bird has been reading Homer?" inquired Jack. Then he added, "He seems to be rather a hermit. Have you seen him with other birds?"

"No."

"So it's a solitary creature?"

"Yes, it seems to spend most of its time alone."

"So it's not just a physical resemblance to you?"

"No, maybe not, but I don't know."

"It's your trial, Abraham."

"What do you mean?"

"I mean that you are doomed to a life of sorrow in this vale of tears. You are the heartiest of fellows, and yet you often feel painfully alone. Maybe this God that you don't believe in figured out that you'd need a heron to keep you company and protect you."

"It's very strange."

"Well, Abe, it may be that He's taking care of an infidel. He's probably still hoping you'll come around. In the meantime, you are going to have to do something to earn your daily bread."

⁂

I accepted the appointment to work for Calhoun as the deputy surveyor of Sangamon County. For Calhoun, the recommendations of my friends had trumped my Whig politics. I remembered from reading Mr. Weems's biography of George Washington that he had been a surveyor. Comparing me to General Washington was pretty farfetched, but it still made me proud to be doing something he had done.

I obtained copies of both Gibson's and Flint's manuals on surveying and studied them carefully with Mentor. Mentor was at his best when he was teaching math, and we spent hours poring over geometry, logarithms, and trigonometry. Sarah put a stop to these sessions at midnight by ordering us to bring in the firewood for the next day.

I became a competent surveyor. Performing in the field helped me improve my skills. I was making enough money to support myself in New Salem—and to begin paying off the notes for the buildings and inventories of both Lincoln and Berry stores.

My friend Henry McHenry recommended me to his neighbors as a surveyor who could help them settle a not unfriendly, but intense, dispute over where the lines of their properties formed a corner. They used the most recent county survey to solve this issue, but to no avail.

On the day we chose for the surveying, I wore a woolen shirt and blue denim pants, which were foxed with buckskin in several places. I was accompanied by Henry and the two disputants as I pulled a chain through thick patches of briars and brush.

Henry was helping me with the chain. I carried my compass and my flagstaff. Normally a surveyor would use a horse on these projects, but I was my own "hoss."

Henry pulled the chain through a tangled patch of old and sturdy briars. The other two men followed him. I directed Henry to crawl slightly to the right. The mass of root, stem, and foliage appeared to be lightening. As Henry covered his head and eyes and pushed forward, his head popped through the brush and into a brilliant panorama of brown prairie grass.

"Abe," called Henry with surprise, "we've come through the brush and into the prairie grass again."

"Well, that's something we didn't expect—so much the better. You fellas carry the chain straight into the field, and I'll come around to the side and then sight from there. I think we're only a couple of hundred yards from the corner."

"I'll believe that when I see it," said one of Henry's neighbors.

"Oh, I think you'll see it, alright," I said.

I sighted for them and then directed them to carry the chain forward along the line I was plotting.

"Stop!" I yelled. They pulled the chain tight and waited for me.

When I joined them, I pointed with my flagstaff to a spot in the field where the roots of the grass were thin.

"Gentlemen, here is the corner," I declared.

Both neighbors laughed at Henry and me.

"Henry," said one, "we're being taken advantage of by this simpleton. I've had more luck with a touched man and a stick looking for where to put my well than we've had with this ne'er-do-well. All he's done is get us scratched up and stuck by every pricker in creation. We'll not pay him a cent."

"Hold on, boys," replied Henry.

I began to dig through the roots of the grass and into the soil beneath them. Surely the original surveyors' mark should still be buried there. I needed to find it to prove my calculations were correct. While Henry watched earnestly, the others began a conversation about the recent harvest, and then they continued with what kind of a winter they were expecting.

At this point, I cried out that I had found something.

Henry's neighbors rushed over, and one said, "Why, I'll be . . ."

As I dug farther, I uncovered six to eight inches of a sharpened stake. I pulled this out and then told Henry and his neighbors to look at the bottom of the hole. There they saw a piece of charcoal, an unmistakable marker placed there by the Rector brothers, who had surveyed the land almost fifteen years earlier.

I was successful in this new profession, but my eyes were on something greater.

It was the summer and time for me to campaign again for a seat in the state legislature. This time I had a chance to win. I wanted a campaign that would introduce me to as many voters as possible before election day.

In July, Rowan Herndon invited me to meet the men and women from Island Grove, a small town just to the west of Springfield. He had moved to Island Grove because, after he shot and killed his wife by accident, he was shunned by the villagers in New Salem and decided to leave.

The mid-July day that Row had chosen for my visit was surprisingly cool. Nonetheless, the thirty men who were scything in the field near Row's house were all working up a healthy sweat. As I approached them, Row asked me if I wanted to make a speech. I declined, and after Row introduced me, I started to shake hands with the men.

One of the men muttered, "I ain't votin' for no one who cain't do the work same as us."

I overheard this and said loudly, "Boys, if that is all, then I am sure of your votes."

I asked the fellow if I could borrow his scythe and pitched into the work of cutting the hay. I led the men in their task for over an hour.

When I returned his scythe, the ornery fellow said apologetically, "Well, Abe Lincoln, you done more than any of us. You won my vote fair and square."

A week before the election, I visited with John Todd Stuart in Springfield. Stuart and I had been together in the Black Hawk War. He was running for re-election to the legislature, and in this election the division between the Jacksonian Democrats and the Henry Clay Whigs was deeper than it was two years earlier. The Democrats were eager to defeat Stuart. Bowling Green came to me with a proposal. Once again there were thirteen candidates for four seats. They would abandon support for two of their candidates and rally behind me for the legislature in the hope of edging out Stuart. Since Stuart was confident he would win one of the seats, he told me to accept the Democrats' offer.

On August 4, 1834, I was elected to the Illinois state legislature with 1,376 votes. I came in second place among the candidates. John Todd Stuart was also elected by placing fourth.

It had taken two years, but I had fulfilled the promise Mr. Rutledge and the other leaders of New Salem saw in me. I had achieved their goal by winning election to the state legislature. I would take my seat ready to represent the interests of the men and women of Sangamon County.

CHAPTER ELEVEN

YOU SHALL NOT RAIN UPON HER GRAVE

I hear the loved survivors tell
How nought from death could save,
Till every sound appears a knell,
And every spot a grave.

The stagecoach wobbled across the primitive prairie road. It was the late fall of 1835. The trees had shed their leaves, and the prairie grass had turned golden brown. A solitary red-tailed hawk floated above the waves of undulating grass. As I peered out of the carriage window, I wondered if we might not simply be swallowed up by the vastness of this brown ocean. "How alone we are in the midst of all this," I thought to myself.

The four of us in the carriage had recently been elected to the state legislature of Illinois, and we were traveling the seventy-five miles from Springfield to the state capital of Vandalia. We left Springfield on the morning of November 28, and we would arrive in Vandalia at 4:00 p.m. the next day. Though our quarters were cramped, and although two of us were Democrats and two were Whigs, we became good friends during the long journey.

As the dusty coach entered Vandalia, we noticed the town's log houses. Entering the town square, the driver blew loudly on a horn to signal the arrival of the mail. He pulled to a stop in front of the post office.

The first to emerge from the carriage was a well-dressed, slim, handsome man with an air of confidence and ease. He was my friend John Todd Stuart, a lawyer from Springfield, who was the leader of the Whigs, the minority party in the legislature. Next to step out were John Dawson and William Carpenter, both farmers and Democrats. I came last in a new blue jean suit, which I had purchased with a loan from my friend Coleman Smoot.

Stuart helped to ease my anxieties. He volunteered to show me the ropes in the legislature, and he asked me to room with him in a Vandalia boardinghouse.

As we walked to our residence, we sighted the capitol. I was surprised by how run-down it looked.

Stuart saw the disappointment on my face.

"Didn't you know?" he asked. "The first building burnt to the ground. These people here are worried that the state capital will be snatched from them."

"Rightly so," I interjected.

"Well, that said," continued Stuart, "they rebuilt it too quickly. They've redone some of it, but it's falling apart. It's an albatross, and they can't figure out what to do with it. Even if they spend the money to replace it, there's no guarantee that they'll keep the capital."

"When does that issue come up again?" I asked.

"They think it will be in the '36–'37 session," replied Stuart.

We walked to the boardinghouse, enjoyed a leisurely dinner, and turned in early to be ready for the opening session in the morning.

Early the next day, Stuart took me for a tour of the capitol. As we walked through the front door of the brick building, we found ourselves in a space that occupied the entire first floor. This was the meeting room of the House of Representatives to which we had been elected.

The room was sparsely furnished. Much of the space was taken by rectangular tables surrounded by chairs— some of which appeared to be more comfortable than others. One table, toward the opposite side of the room, was raised slightly higher than the others; it stood on a modest platform. There were inkstands on each table, candleholders around the room, and a water pail with tin cups on a small table near the door. Throughout the room were small droppings of mortar and plaster from the walls and the ceiling of the decaying building.

At noon the speaker convened the first meeting of the Ninth General Assembly of the Illinois legislature. Three representatives sat at each table. The first order of business was the introduction of the thirty-six new members of the House. We were joined by nineteen returning members. Half of the representatives were farmers and one-quarter of them were lawyers. For much of the first day, the speaker reviewed the rules and procedures of the chamber. He was occasionally interrupted by a piece of falling plaster.

As the first weeks flew by, I found myself more and more at home. Though I had much to learn and spent most of my time listening and absorbing—inside the House but also outside it—I quickly recognized that I could hold my own with any of my colleagues. After hours, we continued to debate the issues, often by the boardinghouse fireplace. I could see this was the lifeblood of politics—having principles, but also being willing to find agreement.

Few of my opinions reached the official record for the winter legislative session, but there is one point on which I did speak up. Upon the news that the surveyor for Schuyler County had died, the legislature appointed a replacement. When they learned that the report had been false, I counseled my fellow representatives to let "matters remain as they were, so that if the old surveyor should hereafter conclude to die, there would be a new one ready made without troubling the legislature."

———

In the spring of 1835, I returned to New Salem from the legislative session in Vandalia. As the first yellow-green emerged in the Illinois prairie countryside—in the fields, the brush, and the trees of the river valley—I walked two or three times a week from New Salem to the Rutledge family farm in Sandridge. This was a journey that took me several miles north of New Salem. As I walked alone to the north in the early afternoon, I was full of excitement and expectation. As I walked alone to the south in the twilight or the darkness of evening, I felt deliriously happy.

On a warm April afternoon, Ann and I were walking along the edge of the Rutledge farm. The green shoots of the prairie grass were springing up through the brown tufts that Ann's brothers had scythed close to the ground the previous fall. Cardinals, blue jays, and goldfinches flew overhead, gathering materials for their nests. A large crow cawed belligerently from the top of a nearby oak, claiming that he had chosen the rights to that particular spot. A raccoon scurried ahead of us into the brush.

Ann stopped for a moment and looked up at me.

"What was Vandalia like?" she asked.

"It took some getting used to, but Stuart helped me," I replied.

"You return next December?"

"Yes."

"What will you do until then?"

"I will study law. Stuart has given me his law books. It's not as easy as grammar, Annie."

"Robert says you write it all down. He says you don't just memorize it, but that you put it in your own words."

"Yes, I can do only a few pages of Blackstone a day. It's a big book and Stuart says I should go through it twice. When I finish that, I have to do Chitty's *Pleadings*, Greenleaf's *Evidence*, and Story's *Equity Jurisprudence*."

We walked a little further, and then with concern in her face and voice, she asked, "How will you get by?"

"Thanks to Uncle Jimmy, I can start surveying again."

"Uncle Jimmy Short who lives over there?" she asked, pointing to the neighboring farm.

"Yes, he's been a good friend. He paid $120 to buy back my instruments. The notes for my half of the store came due and my possessions were attached. For some reason, they didn't take my horse. You know that Berry died in January, and his notes have also come due."

"But then you are free of them."

"I will pay them as well."

Looking up at me, she said, "You are very good to do that, Abe."

"Annie, what about Jacksonville?"

"I will start in the fall. Father has promised me."

"That's wonderful," I replied.

As we strolled on, I reached for her hand. She took mine into her own and pressed it with warmth and tenderness.

180

"Have you heard from him?" I asked.

"No," she responded. "It's now been almost two years. Father and Mother say he has forgotten me and that I have no obligation to him."

"What do you think?"

"Oh, Abe, I'm so happy when I'm with you. You are so kind to me. I didn't know him well, and then we learned he was false to us. He was so successful, but now you are as well. Have you spoken to Father?"

"We've talked about your going to Jacksonville and my future. Your father was the first man to propose me for the legislature. I always listen to his advice."

I paused for a moment and then continued, "He says we can become engaged after you've been at Jacksonville for a year and I've finished my law study."

"That means a year from now, Abe. Can you wait?"

"Of course I can, Annie."

On a June morning, I walked down to the river carrying a large black book under my left arm. I found Kelso's canoe and paddled over to the east bank. Although all the trees had been cut down on both sides of the river, a large oak, a lone watchman, remained on the far side. I steered for this tree, landed the canoe, hid it under the brush, and climbed up the bank. Unlike the spring, when it rained every day, this was a morning of clear air and bright sunshine. I chose to sit under the oak tree for shade.

I began my morning study by bolstering myself against the tree. When my back began to ache, I flattened it on the ground and propped my legs up against the tree trunk. The oak tree and I merged to form an enormous sundial.

Holding my book directly above me, I could read and study tolerably well. In Blackstone's *Commentaries* on this particular day, I was studying "The Rights of Things" and "Of Things Personal."

When I began, I heard a loud splash and then a louder "rok, rok" as a heron landed on the water and then stood up on the shore just below the oak tree. I read the text aloud, recast the words, and then repeated them several times. The bird worked the river pools as thoroughly as I was digging into Blackstone.

I was not disturbed by the heron's movements, and in fact welcomed them, since I never had any company when I studied the law. I was also surprised to glimpse a familiar form walking toward me. Shielding my eyes from the sunbeams, I could see the silhouette of a medium-sized man with a pot belly and sprigs of hair dancing out from the sides of his head.

"Yo, ho, young legislator with your faithful companion!" came Jack Kelso's cheerful cry. "Be careful your brains do not dry up in this prairie sun."

"Jack, my friend!" I shouted. "I am doing my best to shelter them from the sun and the dull Blackstone."

I paused for him to sit near the tree.

"Listen to this," I said reading from Blackstone:

"Under the name of things personal are included all sorts of things moveable, which may attend a man's person wherever he goes; nor paid so much regard to by the law, as things that are in their nature more permanent and immoveable, as lands, and houses, and the profits issuing thereout."

"Enough, my worthy friend. Tell me, is my 'all sorts of things moveable,' by which I mean my canoe, available for my use?"

"It is indeed. I hid it under the brush. But Jack, how did you come to be here and your 'all sorts of things moveable' there"—I pointed across the river—"where I found it this morning?"

"Ah, young friend, it is one of life's mysteries."

"Is the mystery that you can walk on water?"

"Oh, sadly no," he said mournfully. "I suspect it was a potion of earthly form."

Before I could respond, he added, "And now, ferryman, can you take me to yonder shore?"

"I can indeed," I replied. "It's time for me to leave as well."

"For your walk to Sandridge?"

I nodded yes.

"Ah, thy fair maiden," he replied wistfully.

Annie and I had eaten supper with her family and then gone for an early evening walk near the fenced-in pasture of the Rutledge farm. The rain had lifted, but water dripped from the trees onto us. It did not bother us.

Small greenish-yellow sparks flashed through the undergrowth and up into a nearby band of trees. One or two climbed higher and higher toward the tops of the highest evergreens. It was a peculiar night. On an evening when we were comfortable expressing our love for each other, the sound of the water dripping down into last year's leaves caused us to feel earthbound, while the sparks of the fireflies lifted our spirits heavenward.

We walked slowly, and Annie nestled into the warmth of my strong chest and upper arms. I felt free from the earthly bonds that both cheered and plagued me each day. My life unfolded before me. I would become a lawyer, perhaps continue in politics, and settle in to family life with Annie. I looked forward to being a father. My own childhood and family life had been marked by tension and loss; it was Sally's love that had rescued me from the hatred that had built between Papa and me. Annie and I would change all that. It was a vision that gladdened me. In the bosom of a loving family, I could live with the peculiar melancholy that occasionally drifted over me.

Annie broke the spell by raising the only unsettled thing.

"Abe, I won't feel right about it unless I tell him face to face. I know that my family says we should go ahead and marry anyway, but it's just not right."

She looked up at me and said calmly, "I will write him that my affections have changed, but I will ask to see him before we marry."

Rain continued to beat down on the soggy prairie. Without steady sunshine and with waterlogged roots, the vegetables in our gardens were stunted, and the flowers withered and died.

In mid-July, the rains ceased, and the sun began to bake the countryside. Excessive rain was followed by extreme warmth. The sweltering heat and humidity favored the onset of insects and disease.

In August, people began to take ill. The cause was brain fever. It generally lasted four weeks. At first came a low temperature with headaches, but it was followed by high fever, dehydration, and delirium. In some cases, overall weakening was followed by death.

In Springfield, the number of cases overwhelmed the physicians. New Salem was more fortunate, and fewer people came down with the illness. There was no apparent reason why some towns were more affected than others.

Each day I continued to walk to the Rutledge farm.

Her brothers and sisters were spared the illness, but Annie had a low fever and headaches, and she was unable to eat or sleep.

"Abe," she said, "please don't worry. I'll be better in a few days. I'm not ill very often. When the fevers came last year and the year before, everyone else in the family was sick but me. It's just a touch of what's going around."

I held her hand and kissed her on the forehead.

Then came the news that shocked us all.

Ann had received a letter from McNamar telling her that he was coming back to New Salem and that he expected her to marry him. He had stopped off in Cincinnati to buy some things for their house. He had brought his family with him, and they all expected to settle in New Salem.

One afternoon, I found Robert and David at work in the field by the farmhouse. They were beginning to scythe the dwarfed brown grass. The work was proceeding quickly, and they were thankful given the broiling August heat.

They paused from their labors and leaned on the handles of their scythes.

As I walked toward them, I could hear part of their conversation.

". . . It doesn't mean she has to die," said David.

"True, the ones who are dying are the babies and the old folk," responded Robert.

"She is strong, she is young, and no one is more cheerful than Annie," continued David. "Have you ever noticed how the gloomy and drunken people are the sickly ones?"

"No, David, I wish I could agree with you, but I can't. Seems to me that illness comes and goes by chance, and some of those drunkards live past eighty."

I came closer and they greeted me. They told me that Annie had not improved and then about McNamar's letter.

"He's got some nerve to do that," said David angrily. "He's been gone for three years. She hasn't heard from him in almost two years, and then he writes to say he's coming back to marry her. What is she supposed to make of that?"

"Abe," Robert replied kindly, "we'd be hoping that you and Annie would be married before anything like this happened."

"We all know that she wanted to tell him before we got married," I said.

"I don't know," observed Robert, "but on top of that fever, I'm sure she's mighty upset."

Annie was resting in a bedroom toward the rear of the farmhouse. Her favorite cousin, James McGrady Rutledge, had been with her since mid-morning. As he came out of her room, he ushered me in.

Her face was pale. Her healthy coloring was gone.

"Abe," she said, "what should I do?"

"The first thing you must do, Annie, is put it out of your mind."

"You know me well enough, my dear, to know I can't do that."

I reached for her hands.

"Annie, you must clear your mind and rest."

"I know, dearest, but it is hard for me."

"You need to think of what you will learn at Jacksonville in the fall. It's something I've never had the chance to do."

She looked up approvingly at me and said, "I'll never be able to do what you have done by yourself. You are so dedicated to your learning. The family is worried about your health."

"Then, Annie, let us do something for each other. You clear your mind and rest, and I will take more walks with you and put Blackstone aside for awhile."

"That's very sweet of you, Abe. You know I love our walks."

As I held her hands, she faded into a fitful rest.

She did not improve. I knew now that she was in danger, but I had faith in her sturdy constitution.

I believed our love would carry her through. I was convinced of that.

A week later the fever rose and sweat streamed down her face and neck. She was almost too weak to talk. She was a deathly white. At times she was calm, but at others, frenzied and delirious. She would call out "Abe," but when I responded, it was clear that she did not know me. I did not want to believe it, but each day she was receding from me. I could do nothing to help her. When I held her hands, she writhed restlessly with sweat pouring off her, and then I wept.

On August 25, 1835, she died.

———

On a cold and foggy day, I walked down to the river. Through the thick mist I glimpsed the canoe, paddled it to the other side, and pulled myself up the muddy bank. The raw air felt unpleasant as I began to walk through the dead stalks of the brown prairie grass. I did not know where I was going. I did not care.

For several weeks, my friends had been concerned about me, but I'd had no desire to talk to them. Jack Kelso tried to draw me out, but it was no use. Mentor and Sarah Graham offered me dinner or supper, but I did not accept. Sam Hill and Dr. Allen tried to talk to me, but I walked out of the store. I could tell that Bill Greene was watching me, but Bill was easy to elude. The Rutledge family invited me to stay with them, but I declined.

I realized I was walking in the direction of Sandridge and her grave. I looked up at the dark lowering clouds, at the gray-white wisps of fog that blanketed the river valley, and at the black trees divesting themselves of their dead brown leaves.

"You shall not rain upon her grave, nor snow and sleet upon her final resting place, nor storm upon her tomb," I yelled at the threatening clouds.

I looked down at the ground.

"They are worried I will take my own life, but I will not. I am cursed to continue this miserable, wretched existence."

I addressed the words of a poem I knew to the trees and the river and the open field.

Oh! Why should the spirit of mortal be proud?
Like a swift-fleeting meteor, a fast-flying cloud,
A flash of the lightning, a break of the wave,
Man passeth from life to his rest in the grave.

The leaves of the oak and the willow shall fade,
Be scattered around, and together be laid;
And the young and the old, and the low and the high
Shall molder to dust and together shall lie.

———

The maid on whose cheek, on whose brow, in whose eye,
Shone beauty and pleasure—her triumphs are by . . .

———

Nancy and Bowling Green took me in. I stayed in their upstairs room. There was a bed, a chest, and a chair. The rafters hung down. It was dark most of the time.

There was little color in the room. It was deep brown

and black. I slept most of the day and night.

When I was not asleep, I stared at the ceiling. I could not direct my thoughts. The pictures in my mind were of my mother, my sister, and Ann. They were always before me.

One morning I heard Bowling Green climbing the stairs. The steps creaked from his bulk, and I could hear his labored breathing.

He entered the room, pulled the chair near the bed, and collapsed into it. If he had tried to sit on the end of the bed, he would have crushed it.

"Abe," he said, "is there anything we can do?"

"No."

"You have no idea how worried we are about you."

I did not reply.

"We are afraid you may take your own life," he continued.

I said nothing.

"You must try to eat," he said softly.

"You need not worry," I said flatly.

"Abe, we have all known grief. We have all lost parents, sisters, brothers, husbands, wives, children, and friends. Each one beloved. With the loss of each, our hold on life loosens. You have the choice to join them, but you have the choice to remain with us."

I did not reply.

"Abe, remember that Hamlet lets his grief destroy him. He is a good man who cannot act."

I said nothing.

"It can destroy you, Abe."

"I cannot bear the thought of leaving nothing behind, nothing for anyone to know that I have lived," I said.

Nancy had climbed the stairs. She entered the room. She sat beside me on the bed. She placed her hand on my forehead.

"Abe," she said, "please come down and eat."

Slowly I pulled myself up, swung my legs around, and placed my feet on the floor. I arose and walked quietly down the stairs with her.

CHAPTER TWELVE

A FATAL PATH THROUGH THE BRAIN

I range the fields with pensive tread,
And pace the hollow rooms,
And feel (companion of the dead)
I'm living in the tombs.

G radually, I recovered from the loss of Ann. There were pieces of my life that helped me to re-establish routines. Once again, I immersed myself in my law studies. To add to my income, I continued to survey plots in Petersburg. I was still a member of the state legislature and would return to session in the late fall.

When the legislature reconvened in Vandalia, I became more active in promoting the Whig agenda. We designed a plan for reworking the Sangamon into a canal from Beardstown to Springfield to foster commerce. I became more active in the leadership of our party. The following summer I ran for re-election.

On election day, August 1, 1836, I placed first among sixteen candidates for the state legislature. In the 1836–37 session, I was elected the leader of the Whig party. I was one of a group of Sangamon legislators who were called "the Long Nine" because we were all over six feet tall. We were instrumental in moving the state capital from Vandalia to Springfield. This foreshadowed a major change that would be occurring in my life.

In September 1836, I was licensed by the Illinois Supreme Court to practice law in Illinois. When John Todd Stuart extended me an invitation to become his partner, I accepted, and in April 1837 the law firm of Stuart and Lincoln was established in Springfield.

A national economic collapse in 1837 ended any possibility for reconstructing the Sangamon River. New Salem's decline, feared by some since the mid-1830s, accelerated. Most of the residents had already relocated to Petersburg. I would be moving to Springfield.

In the summer of 1831, I had come to New Salem as a piece of floating driftwood. Six years later, I set out for Springfield, the new capital of Illinois, as a member of the state legislature and as a licensed lawyer ready to begin practice. I had become the Telemachus who stood by his father's side and slew the suitors.

My mentors were my friends in New Salem. From Mentor Graham, I learned that language had structure and rhythm and that mathematics was logical and precise. From Jack Kelso, I learned to understand my nature—that I would always be engaged but often alone. From James Rutledge, I learned to welcome and trust my ambition. From Bowling Green, I learned that the law was the fabric that held a community together. From Annie, I learned that I could heal, although, in the death of another, a part of me would die as well.

I had developed the confidence to grow on my own, and it was time for me to begin a new life in Springfield.

Before I left, I wanted to walk once more through the fields and forests on the east side of the river. However painful, I wished to revisit the places where Annie and I had wandered together at the height of our happiness. I wanted to fix her memory in my heart and to carry her with me. I could think of her now without allowing the heavy melancholy to envelop me.

I had said my goodbyes to Sam and Parthena Hill, to Hardin Bale, to Henry Onstot, and to the Trent family. Jack Kelso, Rowan Herndon, Bill Greene, Jack and Hannah Armstrong, Henry McHenry, "Uncle Jimmy"

Short, and the Rutledges had all left. When Jack Kelso left New Salem, he gave me his canoe.

I walked down the hill to set out in the canoe. I noticed how quiet it was. New Salem had once been a bustling frontier village. Children no longer played along the bank. The water still rushed over the dam, but the mill was not grinding this April morning. The early spring flowers still dotted the hillside.

As I paddled across the river, a melancholy mood settled over me. I was not surprised. It was something I had expected, but I had decided to make this visit anyway.

Because the canoe had little value, I rarely hid it in the brush on the far side. Perhaps out of habit, I lifted the larger branches of a low-lying evergreen.

It took a few seconds for me to grasp what lay in front of me. Just under the branches was a large bundle of gray-blue feathers stretched out upon the ground. The head rested on the soil. The yellow-brown bill brushed up against the dark-brown bark of the tree. The one eye that I could see was closed.

I knew what it was. I had not seen it recently.

My feelings shut down once more. I had nothing left to feel. I stepped forward and lifted the soft clump of feathers from the ground. I cradled the neck and head so it would not hang down, but the legs and feet dangled limply from my arms. I carried it out to the riverbank and laid it gently on the grass.

As I set it down, I noticed something odd. Since the head had been resting on its left side, I had not seen the blood caked into the white feathers underneath it. I probed the blotch of reddish brown, and it revealed a small but distinct hole piercing into the upper left of the head. There was no mark on the right side of the skull. The bullet entered through the back of the head on the left side, traced a fatal path through the brain, and lodged near the right eye. The heron died suddenly, and except for a split second, painlessly.

Later in the day, I borrowed a spade from Henry Onstot and crossed the river once more. I chose a grave near the place where I first saw the heron flying overhead when we arrived in New Salem on the flatboat. The digging into the caked earth was slow. Gradually, with each shovelful of soil, the pile of earth grew larger. I wanted to dig deep enough so that no scavenger could disturb the heron's rest.

When I reached a proper depth, I placed the heron carefully on its side. I started to shovel the soil into the grave. The first lumps rested on its gray feathers, and before long the earth covered it. I paused and looked over the river up toward the vacant buildings of the town. Then I filled the grave, evened out the ground on top, and crossed back over the river.

Acknowledgments

Ten years ago, my friend and colleague at Mary Institute and St. Louis Country Day School (MICDS), Caroline Leonard, urged me to write a young adult novel about Abraham Lincoln. I began in earnest seven years ago, and there are several close friends whose guidance and support kept me going during times of doubt and discouragement.

In one of my many journeys to the Abraham Lincoln Book Shop in Chicago, I came across a book titled *Reading with Lincoln* by Robert Bray. It is a first-rate study of Lincoln's intellectual development. I commended the book and its author to my readers in a piece in the *St. Louis Post-Dispatch* on Lincoln's birthday. After Bob Bray emailed me, we met and have been good friends ever since. To have the counsel of a Lincoln scholar during the writing of *Young Lincoln* was a gift. Bob's kindness and humility were an inspiration for me.

To Josh Stevens, the founder of Reedy Press, and my daughter Jorie Jacobi, I owe the key decision to change the narrative to first person. I resisted for months, and finally, when I tried it, the story flowed as it had not before. Josh is a gifted publisher, and his unvarnished critiques often provoked angst as well as an improved narrative. Kathleen Dragan, my editor at Reedy Press, while conveying her belief in the story, firmly pushed me to improve it again and again. I am deeply grateful for her persistence and expertise.

I read selections from the manuscript to my eighth-grade English students at MICDS. Of course, they liked the wrestling match and the story of Lincoln's grandfather being killed by an Indian, but some of them listened attentively to the descriptions and the quieter moments when Lincoln is reflecting to himself. They gave me helpful suggestions for revision.

I thank my niece Nina Jacobi, my sister-in-law Nancy Newton, and my friends Bob Wiltenburg, Candace O'Connor, Jack Klobnak, Caroline Leonard, and Pat Moffat for reading the manuscript, critiquing it, and giving me encouragement.

Without the love and support of my wife, Ginger, I could not have written this story. She is a fierce guardian of our time together and of our family time with our children, and she graciously accepted my need to spend hours in the Clayton library. We take our three dogs for walks around Washington University, and knowing that I was writing about Lincoln and his dog, Honey, may have helped my cause.

Author Source Notes

This is a work of fiction.

It is, of course, about someone who lived and about whom many splendid biographies and histories have been written.

By adapting the historical material and the reliable Lincoln stories to a first-person treatment of his life, I have taken the liberties that only fiction can provide.

I have relied on a number of primary and secondary sources.

I could not have written this book, if Douglas Wilson and Rodney Davis had not spent years compiling the reminiscences of Lincoln that William H. Herndon collected shortly after the president's assassination. Their work, *Herndon's Informants* (University of Illinois, 1998), has been my bible. I must also acknowledge my debt to Douglas Wilson's award-winning book, *Honor's Voice* (1999), which is a study of Lincoln in New Salem and his early years in Springfield. Michael Burlingame's *Abraham Lincoln: A Life* (2008) has also been an indispensable source.

I do want the reader to know there are places in the text where the words are not my own. While most of what Lincoln thinks and says is what I believe he could have thought and said, in some places the words he speaks are actually his. When Lincoln tells Anna Roby about the moon, those are his words as recalled by Anna

Roby in her reminiscence given to Herndon; Lincoln's campaign speech to the citizens of Pappsville includes the well-known quote that his "policies are short and sweet like the old woman's dance"; When called upon to be a character witness in Bowling Green's courtroom, Lincoln testified, "He is called lying Pete Lukins." None of these could have been paraphrased but to the detriment of the story.

Even though this work is fictional, I have relied on a number of primary and secondary sources, and there are places where I do want to give credit to others. These I have identified in the notes below.

The brief headnotes for each chapter but one are excerpts from two of Lincoln's poems: "My Childhood Home I See Again" and "The Bear Hunt." The headnote for Chapter 5 is a short poem Lincoln wrote in his childhood arithmetic book.

I have been reading and writing about Lincoln for almost thirty years. I stand on the shoulders of giants. I am indebted to them all. If my "poor power to add or detract" contributes to a student's enjoyment and understanding of our greatest president, it comes not so much from me as it does from the many scholars and writers upon whom I have relied.

Sources

Abbreviations and Short Titles Employed in Notes

Burlingame, *AL: A Life*: Michael Burlingame, *Abraham Lincoln: A Life, Volume One* (Baltimore: Johns Hopkins University Press, 2008).

CW: *The Collected Works of Abraham Lincoln*, 9 vols., ed. Roy P. Basler (New Brunswick, NJ: Rutgers University Press, 1953–55).

Fehrenbacher, *Recollected Words*: Don E. Fehrenbacher and Virginia Fehrenbacher, eds., *Recollected Words of Abraham Lincoln* (Stanford, CA: Stanford University Press, 1996).

HI: Douglas L. Wilson and Rodney O. Davis, eds., *Herndon's Informants: Letters, Interviews, and Statements about Abraham Lincoln* (Urbana: University of Illinois Press, 1998).

Preface

VII "Just think of such a sucker…" David Herbert Donald, *Lincoln* (New York: Simon and Schuster, 1995), 235.

VII "One fellow told me…" J. Rowan Herndon to WHH (letter), May 28, 1865, *HI*, 7.

Part One
Chapter One

4 "I was six and Mama was off…" Dennis F. Hanks to WHH (interview), June 13, 1865, *HI*, 36.

6 "The cabin was dark and close . . . ." Burlingame, *AL: A Life*, 15.

6 "One night the only thing…" Fehrenbacher, *Recollected Words*, 299.

7 "I remember when my toes…" Burlingame, *AL: A Life*, 16.

7 "Once I came across…" Burlingame, *AL: A Life*, 11.

9 "One Saturday afternoon…" Fehrenbacher, *Recollected Words*, 508.

13 "Papa's face turned bright red…" Dennis F. Hanks to WHH (letter), January 26, 1866, *HI*, 176.

13 "I heard they got rid of…" Paul Schneider, *Old Man River* (New York: Henry Holt, 2014), 231.

15 "At one crossing, Austin said…" Charles Friend to WHH (letter), March 19, 1866, *HI*, 235.

17 "Well, what I don't git…" J. Rogers Gore, *The Boyhood of Abraham Lincoln* (Indianapolis: Bobbs-Merrill, 1921), 275.

17 "One afternoon…" Burlingame, *AL: A Life*, 18.

Chapter Two

25 "It turned out…" Burlingame, *AL: A Life*, 20.

28 "Papa built..." Burlingame, *AL: A Life*, 22.

29 "A flock of wild turkeys..." *CW*, 4:62.

34 "Mama told him..." Burlingame, *AL: A Life*, 25.

35 "she called us to her side..." Dennis F. Hanks to WHH (interview), June 13, 1865, *HI*, 40.

36 "Papa had built the coffins..." Burlingame, *AL: A Life*, 25.

Chapter Three

43 "She stroked..." Burlingame, *AL: A Life*, 27.

44 "The first thing..." Burlingame, *AL: A Life*, 28.

46 "It was Mr. Weems's book..." *CW*, 4:235.

48 "until one of you spells this word...defied." Burlingame, *AL: A Life*, 32.

50 "Papa was always on the short end..." Burlingame, *AL: A Life*, 42.

50 "It was when I was working for..." Burlingame, *AL: A Life*, 37.

51 "Abe, you can clown real good..." Burlingame, *AL: A Life*, 40.

52 "It was one thing to be funny..." Fehrenbacher, *Recollected Words*, 236–237.

54 "Ain't you the one..." Matilda Johnston Moore to WHH (interview), September 8, *HI*, 109.

54 "When I was seventeen..." Burlingame, *AL: A Life*, 42.

Chapter Four

60 "Allen pointed out something to me." *CW*, 3:455.

60 "Pretty soon we came to the place..." Richard Campanella, *Lincoln in New Orleans* (University of Louisiana at Lafayette Press, 2010), 62.

62 "the Shaking of Earth." Dennis F. Hanks to WHH (letter), March 7, 1866, *HI*, 227.

62 "I thought I heard rustling..." *CW*, 4:62.

64 "Lincoln, get the guns and shoot." Anna Caroline Gentry to WHH (interview), September 17, 1865, *HI*, 131.

65 "When we drifted into the harbor..." Campanella, *Lincoln in New Orleans*, 88.

65 "From the docks rose the first smells..." Campanella, *Lincoln in New Orleans*, 94.

66 "I had never been near..." Campanella, *Lincoln in New Orleans*, 94–95.

67 "In Orleans there were newspapers..." Campanella, *Lincoln in New Orleans*, 107–108.

71 "From Sheriff Turnham..." Burlingame, *AL: A Life*, 43.

72 "Colonel Jones owned..." Burlingame, *AL: A Life*, 36.

72 "Lawyer Brackenridge invited..." S. T. Johnson (WHH interview), September 14, 1865, *HI*, 115.

74 "I have nothing left to live for." Burlingame, *AL: A Life*, 45.

75 "Papa wasn't sure…" Burlingame, *AL: A Life*, 46.

76 "You see, I had taken to writing poetry…" Burlingame, *AL: A Life*, 46.

76 "I am the big buck of the lick." Burlingame, *AL: A Life*, 47.

Part Two
Chapter Six

83 "A Piece of Floating Driftwood." William H. Herndon and Jesse W. Weik, *Herndon's Lincoln*, ed. Douglas L. Wilson and Rodney O. Davis (Urbana: University of Illinois Press, 2006), 62.

84 "As we rounded it…" Benjamin P. Thomas, *Lincoln's New Salem* (Carbondale: Southern Illinois University Press, 1987), 59–60.

85 "The bow slid forward and began to scrape…" John Hanks to WHH (interview), June 13, 1865, *HI*, 44.

91 "Good boys who to their books apply…" Joseph C. Richardson to WHH (interview), September 14?, 1865, *HI*, 119.

91 "the strange, uneducated, penniless boy…" *CW*, 1:320.

92 "Back in Indiana one night…" Anna Caroline Gentry to WHH (interview), September 17, 1865, *HI*, 132.

94 "I can make a few rabbit scratches…" Thomas P. Reep, *Abe Lincoln and the Frontier Folk of New Salem* (Middletown, CT: Southfarm Press, 2002), 36.

94 "On election day in Kentucky…" John B. Weber to WHH (letter), November 5, 1866, *HI*, 396.

97 "Row Herndon tried to tell us…" Reep, *Abe Lincoln and the Frontier Folk of New Salem*, 19–20.

100 "The next Saturday morning…" Douglas L. Wilson, *Honor's Voice* (New York, Alfred A. Knopf, 1999), Chapter 1, "Wrestling with the Evidence," 19–51.

100 "There'll be no tusslin' and scufflin'…" Henry McHenry to WHH (interview), October 10, 1866, *HI*, 369.

102 "Leg him, Jack." Burlingame, *AL: A Life*, 62.

Chapter Seven

106 "They had the pinkish tint…" Kunigunde Duncan, *Lincoln's Teacher* (Great Barrington, Mass., Advance Pub. Co., 1958), 122.

108 "If I had a grammar book…" Mentor Graham to WHH (interview), May 29, 1865, *HI*, 10.

109 "There was one about a boy and a girl…" Louis A. Warren, *Lincoln's Youth: Indiana Years*, 1816–1830 (Indianapolis: Indiana Historical Society Press, 1959), 41.

113 "Sarah was Mentor's childhood sweetheart."

Duncan, *Lincoln's Teacher*, 89.

115 "The distinction between..." Samuel Kirkham, *Kirkham's Grammar* (Springfield, IL, Octavo Press, 1999), 32.

116 "James Rutledge had established..." Robert B. Rutledge to WHH (letter), November 1, 1866, *HI*, 384–385.

117 "I had little experience speaking in public..." Burlingame, *AL: A Life*, 49.

117 "That same summer..." Burlingame, *AL: A Life*, 50.

119 "As we meet tonight..." *CW*, 1:5–9.

119 "The members of the audience seemed stunned..." Burlingame, *AL: A Life*, 65.

Chapter Eight

125 "Every man is said to have his peculiar ambition." *CW*, 1:8–9.

130 "I'll be damned, Bill..." Burlingame, *AL: A Life*, 67.

131 "Go to the devil, sir." Burlingame, *AL: A Life*, 67.

132 "This company will break ranks..." Burlingame, *AL: A Life*, 67.

133 "...tasted like saddlebags." George M. Harrison to WHH (letter), January 29, 1867, *HI*, 555.

133 "Boys, the man threw me..." William G. Greene to WHH (interview), May 30, 1865, *HI*, 19.

133 "One night soldier Pot Greene..." David M.

Pantier to WHH (letter), July 21, 1865, *HI*, 78.

135 "Twelve bodies…" Royal Clark to WHH (interview), October 1866?, *HI*, 371.

137 "An old Indian…" William G. Greene to WHH (interview), May 30, 1865, *HI*, 19.

Chapter Nine

141 "Fellow citizens, I have been told…" J. Rowan Herndon to WHH (letter), May 28, 1865, *HI*, 7.

142 "Gentlemen, I have just returned…" Henry McHenry to WHH (interview), May 29, 1865, *HI*, 15.

142 "At this point a huge fight broke out…" J. Rowan Herndon to WHH (letter), May 28, 1865, *HI*, 7.

142 "Fellow citizens, I presume you all know…" Abner Y. Ellis (statement for WHH), January 23, 1866, *HI*, 171.

144 "If that is what they call a science…" Wilson, *Honor's Voice*, 95.

146 "He was dressed in a shirt…" J. Rowan Herndon to WHH (letter), July 3, 1865, *HI*, 69.

147 "I do not believe in the creed…" Thomas Paine, *The Age of Reason* (New York: Random House, 2003), 245.

148 "O Thou that in the Heavens…" Burlingame, *AL: A Life*, 84.

149 "I've got Berry in on a plan…" J. Rowan Herndon

to WHH (letter), July 3, 1865, *HI*, 70.

155 "In the early morning hours…" Reep, *Abe Lincoln and the Frontier Folk of New Salem*, 20–21.

Chapter Ten

160 "…he is called Lying Pete Lukins…" J. Rowan Herndon to WHH (letter), July 3, 1865, *HI*, 69.

163 "The two witnesses we have heard…" Burlingame, *AL: A Life*, 86.

163 "The first duty of the court…" Burlingame, *AL: A Life*, 86.

164 "…he recited verses from Burns and soliloquies from Shakespeare…" Caleb Carman to WHH (interview), October 12, 1866, *HI*, 374.

171 "Gentlemen, here is the corner." Henry McHenry to WHH (interview), May 29, 1865, *HI*, 14.

173 "Boys, if that is all…" J. Rowan Herndon to WHH (letter), May 28, 1865, *HI*, 8.

173 "The Democrats were eager to defeat Stuart." Burlingame, *AL: A Life*, 81.

Chapter 11

176 "As the dusty coach entered Vandalia…" William E. Barringer, *Lincoln's Vandalia* (New Brunswick: Rutgers University Press, 1949), 26–27.

176 "The first to emerge…" Barringer, *Lincoln's Vandalia*, 27.

177 "The room was sparsely furnished." Paul Simon, *Lincoln's Preparation for Greatness* (Norman: University of Oklahoma Press, 1965), 21–22.

178 "At noon the speaker convened..." Simon, *Lincoln's Preparation for Greatness*, 20–21.

178 "Upon the news..." Burlingame, *AL: A Life*, 96.

181 "I began my morning study..." Burlingame, *AL: A Life*, 91.

184 "My life unfolded before me." Henry McHenry to WHH (interview), 1866, *HI*, 534.

189 "You shall not rain..." Elizabeth Abell to WHH (letter), February 15, 1867, *HI*, 557.

189 "Nancy and Bowling Green took me in." George U. Miles to WHH, March 23, 1866, *HI*, 236.

From *Lincoln in Springfield*

I first met Mary in the fall of 1839. It was just
before the start of the legislative session, the first one to
be held in Springfield. Ninian and Elizabeth Edwards
hosted gatherings at their large house on Aristocracy
Hill. Douglas, Baker, and Trumbull were often there
along with Mercy Levering, Mary Todd, Catherine
Bergen, and later Ninian's cousin, Matilda Edwards, who
entranced every young man in Springfield. I always went
in the company of my friend Joshua Speed.

I was much taken with Mary. It seemed to me that
she was everything I wasn't. She came from a rich family
in Lexington, Kentucky. Mary could speak French, which
she had learned at Madame Mentelle's Boarding School.
She was lively, charming, and cultured, and she ably
guided our conversations. I was soon at ease listening
to her and just gazing at her pretty face and lovely
complexion.

She knew about politics and poetry. Henry Clay
was the politician I most admired, and Mary Todd
had sat next to him at a dinner party given by her
father in Lexington. She was a passionate Whig and
ardently supported Henry Clay for president. Mary and
I read aloud to each other. One of her favorites was
Robert Burns. She read his poems with feeling, and she

appreciated Burns's sharp wit. She loved to hear me recite "Holy Willie's Prayer" and "Tam O'Shanter."

We continued to see each other at the Edwards' home over the winter and into the spring, although I was frequently away because of my law practice or for political gatherings across the state. In the summer, Mary visited relatives in Missouri, and we corresponded often.

In October, we declared an understanding to each other that we would be married early in 1841.

And then the doubts began.

We were very different. Because Mary was so attentive and engaging when we were courting, I had not focused on our particularities. Would our temperaments be compatible? I began to wonder. What about our backgrounds? She was used to a life of privilege and ease. Could she live happily in one room in a boarding house?

She loved social occasions. I was happier reading the newspapers. She loved to dance. When we courted, I made the mistake of telling her I wanted to dance with her in the worst way. Later I learned she had told Mercy Levering that I had danced in the worst way.

The doubts grew stronger.

Finally I showed Speed a letter I had written telling her I no longer loved her. He convinced me that I must go to her directly, and that I should burn the letter.

At the time, Mary was living with Ninian and Elizabeth. I felt as if I were walking to the gallows, but Speed was right and I had to tell her my feelings had changed. We sat on the sofa in the parlor. I was very uncomfortable, but Mary listened patiently and held back tears. Then she rose and released me.

Somehow she had learned the truth....I was in love with Matilda.